A Sherlock Holmes Alphabet of Cases

Volume 4
(P to T)

From the Notes of
John H. Watson M.D.

Edited by

Roger Riccard

First published in 2020 by
The Irregular Special Press
for Baker Street Studios Ltd
Endeavour House
170 Woodland Road, Sawston
Cambridge, CB22 3DX, UK

ISBN: 1 901091 77 5 (10 digit)
ISBN: 978 1 901091 77 9 (13 digit)

Cover Illustration: Sidney Paget illustration of Holmes from
The Adventure of the Naval Treaty (1893).

Typeset in 8/11/20pt Palatino

About the Author

Roger Riccard has Scottish roots, tracing his lineage back to the Roses of Kilravock Castle in Highland, Scotland. This British Isles ancestry encouraged his interest in the writings of Sir Arthur Conan Doyle. The British Granada television series, *Sherlock Holmes* (1984-1994) starring Jeremy Brett and Edward Hardwicke, further inspired him to craft more adventures of the famous detective. This is the 4th volume in his *Alphabet of Cases* series. He also has two novels and a selection of Holmes Christmas stories to his credit.

He lives in a suburb of Los Angeles, CA U.S.A. with his wife Rosilyn and their 'kids'; Cats named Bela (after Bela Lugosi who played *Dracula*, because he likes to bite) and Amanda (after Amanda Blake who played Miss Kitty on the old television western, *Gunsmoke*). When not editing Watson's Sherlock Holmes adventures, he and his wife are watching baseball, old movies and crime dramas; or singing with a group that entertains seniors in retirement homes.

Other Books by
Roger Riccard

Sherlock Holmes & The Case of the Poisoned Lilly

Sherlock Holmes & The Case of the Twain Papers

Sherlock Holmes: Adventures for the Twelve Days of Christmas

Sherlock Holmes: Further Adventures for the Twelve Days of Christmas

A Sherlock Holmes Alphabet of Cases Volume One: A-E

A Sherlock Holmes Alphabet of Cases Volume Two: F-J

A Sherlock Holmes Alphabet of Cases Volume Three: K-O

To my Rosilyn,
My Rock

Contents

The Piccadilly Poisoner

Chapter One

Shortly after I took up residence with the consulting detective, Mr. Sherlock Holmes, at 221B Baker Street, I found occasion to involve him in a case of a patient I came across while working at St. Bartholomew's Hospital.

The person in question was a young woman named Mrs. Bertram Morgan, *nee* Dinah Patel. She was a dark-haired beauty in her early twenties, with a trim figure and a heart shaped face that set off her doe brown eyes and flashing smile. While she was of Indian descent, her skin tone was of a lighter shade than most of her people, due to her mixed Anglo-Indian parentage.

Her husband was a wealthy East India importer, who was well known for his travels to the Orient and the unique items he was able to provide to the London elite, in addition to his standard imports of teas and spices. He was also nearly twenty-five years older than she, being a widower. His first wife, who was of an equal age to himself, had died of a heart ailment some four years ago. After a suitable year-long mourning period, he began courting Miss Patel, the daughter of one of his Indian suppliers. They married some eight months later, much to the consternation, it was rumoured, of his twenty-year-old son, Whitaker.

Now she was in hospital, complaining of abdominal pain, fever and skin irritation. My questioning of her activities and diet led me to believe she was suffering some type of food poisoning, perhaps brought on by improperly prepared meals of her largely Oriental diet. Therefore, I questioned her about her recent meals and activities.

"These symptoms have been present before over the past several weeks, but the pain was not so great and I thought it may have been my attempt to acclimatise myself to English food. Last night, however, we had a traditional Indian meal. My husband and I had the same dishes and he did not become ill."

"Were there any other persons eating with you? Some guests, perhaps?"

"No, just my stepson, Whitaker. But he does not partake of Indian dishes. He has never developed a taste for our food as his father has. He had a beef stew instead. I think he does these things just to insult me, knowing that I do not eat meat from cows."

I gave her a sympathetic look as she winced in pain, then enquired, "Your stepson is not cordial toward you?"

She frowned in reply, "His prejudice is obvious when we are alone. He never got over the loss of his mother, as if it were my fault she had a heart attack. In public he puts on a show of respect, but that is all and such occasions are rare. Even Bertram and I do not go out together in public often. Usually we just visit his more tolerant friends, who are accepting of our marriage."

Having served with Her Majesty's Army in India, I was well aware of the racial tensions that mixed marriages incurred and a nagging thought found its way to my tongue. "Who prepared your meal last night, Mrs. Morgan?"

"My maidservant, Bala. She has been with me for years, long before my marriage."

"Did anyone else have access to the kitchen?"

"It's certainly not guarded, Doctor. Any of the household staff could come and go as they please. But she is very particular about being left alone to concentrate when she prepares our meals. The staff know not to bother her while she's cooking, so if you are thinking she may have been distracted and did something wrong, I assure you that it's not possible."

Not wishing to overly concern her, I amended the conversation. "Of course, most likely it is just a case of a spoiled ingredient. Or perhaps something entirely different. A bug bite, or some form of bacteria. We'll keep an eye on you for the next day or two and see what transpires."

She looked at me with exasperation in her eyes, "Must I stay here, Doctor? Bala is quite capable of looking after my needs at home."

I sympathized, but preferred to be cautious and replied, "While the symptoms are uncomfortable, it is important that your body expel the poisons. I'm recommending that we keep you here until you feel stronger. I'll have your diet restricted to bland foods and water. You should be up and about tomorrow or the next day."

In spite of my comforting words to the lady, when I left her, I immediately went to the hospital library to consult some medical journals. Her symptoms, thus far, could indicate any number of ailments. However, the fact that she was the only one affected suggested that poison could be involved. Perhaps it was my new daily exposure to the life of Sherlock Holmes, and the criminal elements he dealt with, which was jading my thoughts. For the time being, I resolved to keep an eye on Mrs. Morgan until I was certain she was in no danger.

That evening when I arrived home, I found Holmes in our sitting room in his shirtsleeves. His right hand was soaking in a basin of water filled with Epsom salts and there was a bruise on his left cheek.

"What happened, Holmes? Did one of your cases turn violent?" I enquired.

"Not a case, Doctor," he replied, as he lifted his knuckles from the basin and inspected them before re-submerging them. "I occasionally engage in a bout of fisticuffs to maintain my fighting skills and make a little money on the side to assist with the rent. Unfortunately, today's opponent slipped under one of my jabs to his jaw, causing me to bounce my fist off his rather hard skull. I prevailed in the end by wearing him down, as I avoided his punches over time. By the eighth round he was too tired to keep his guard up and I ended it with a knockout blow."

I stood above him and bent to examine his cheek. My touch brought about a wince and I noted, "It appears you didn't avoid *all* his punches, old chap. Let me get some ice from Mrs. Hudson for that bruise."

After I ministered to Holmes' wound, I sat by the fire and took up an evening paper. Mrs. Morgan was still on my mind, however, and I decided to broach an idea with the detective.

"I say, Holmes, I've observed you consulting your collection of indexes from time to time when you've been on a case. Do you have any file of information on a fellow named Bertram Morgan? He's an importer of Oriental foods and commodities."

He took his hand from the basin and dried it as he replied, "The name is not completely unfamiliar to me, Watson." He rose and stepped over to the shelves where he pulled out a volume in which he had pasted several articles on various people and subjects which he felt may be relevant to his work at some point. Flipping through pages, he finally settled on one and read as follows:

"Morgan, Bertram. Born 1st May 1836. Only child of Henry and Mary (*nee* Reston). Oxford, degree in finance. Married Susannah Concord 10th May 1857. One child, Whittaker Henry, born 25th August 1860. Wife Susannah died of heart attack 2nd February 1878. Remarried Dinah Patel, age 20, daughter of Arjun and Harriet Patel (*née* Osgood), November 1879 in Chennai, India. Importer of spices, coffee, tea and unique Oriental arts and goods. Successfully survived the great coffee rust plague and converted to importing tea. Method and terms of doing so are vague, but no criminal activity has yet come to fore."

"Anything more specific about the son?" I asked.

"I've only recorded the fact of his existence, Watson. He has exhibited no behaviour worth noting, as yet."

He snapped the book shut with his uninjured hand, deposited it on the shelf and returned to his chair, where he took up his pipe and asked, "So what has happened to Mrs. Morgan that merits your inquisition, Doctor?"

"Why did you presume that Mrs. Morgan was the subject of my interest?"

"Your tone when you asked the question," he answered. "Also, when you bent over me to check my cheek, I noticed a distinct scent of jasmine perfume common among Indian women. It was, therefore, likely then that you were in close proximity to such a person. As your character would eliminate such intimacy with a married woman, I deduced that she was a patient of yours."

"As usual, you are correct on all counts, Holmes," I replied. "She was in hospital today with symptoms that could be linked to poisoning. When I questioned her about her home life, she indicated that there was some unpleasant prejudice in their circles which she has had to deal with. She's also especially concerned about her stepson, Whittaker, who has never taken a liking to her."

"A natural occurrence among stepchildren who are closer in age to their new stepmother than their father. Add in the racial factor and the situation is ripe for dissent. Tell me what you know."

I explained what the lady had told me and Holmes puffed thoughtfully on his pipe for several minutes in thought. Finally, he spoke. "There are many ways that poison can be administered, both deliberately and accidentally. If you like, Doctor, I am currently without a case and could look into the matter for you."

"If you would be so good, Holmes," I said. "It would ease my mind and could well assist my diagnosis."

"Consider it done. Now here is what I propose ..."

Chapter Two

By the end of the next day's rounds, Mrs. Morgan was doing much better and I agreed to sending her home. However, I included the caveat that I would be coming around the following day with a specialist who would be looking in on her. She hesitated, but I insisted, and she acquiesced.

The following morning, Holmes and I arrived at the Morgan home in Piccadilly. He had affected mutton chop whiskers and a moustache to disguise himself and hide his boxing bruise. We were greeted at the door by Dugan, a butler of rotund proportions, who spoke with a trace of an Irish accent. He took our hats and coats and showed us into the sitting room, where Mrs. Morgan sat reading a letter by the fire. She was so absorbed in her activity that she reacted with a start when Dugan cleared his throat to announce our presence. Efficiently slipping the letter back into its envelope and then into a book on the end table next to her, she rose and held out her hand in greeting.

I introduced Holmes to Mrs. Morgan as 'Dr. William Scott, an expert in internal medicine'. As Holmes bowed over her hand she declared, Oh, dear ... I do hope I am not causing you so much trouble, Doctor. I am feeling much better today."

"Nonsense!" Holmes declared. "We cannot have such a lovely woman as yourself succumbing to conditions in

London that you would have no worries about in your home country. The Queen's subjects must feel safe wherever they live."

The lady tilted her head in gratitude and invited us to sit down as she asked Dugan to stir up the fire. "I do admit that I like a good warm fire," She said. "This English weather takes much getting used to after growing up in the tropics of my homeland. Would you care for some hot tea, gentlemen?"

We declined her offer, then Holmes continued, "I understand your acclimatisation difficulties completely. Has the chill ever affected your health? Made you more susceptible to catching cold or that sort of thing?"

She looked pensive and then recalled, "I did have a severe cold the winter before last. I took to my bed for several days. But nothing since then, until these latest symptoms. Do you suppose the weather could be the cause, Dr. Scott?"

"Highly unlikely, madam," he answered. "Though I would like to rule out any external factors, if I may. Germs or bacteria could be airborne or transmitted by touch. With your permission, I would examine the kitchen, your bedroom, rooms such as this, where you spend significant time, even your water closet could be a source of this malady."

"Is that really necessary, Doctor?" she asked, appearing sceptical.

"Oh, I assure you, Mrs. Morgan, I have found breeding grounds for disease in the most unlikely of places."

She pondered that as she sat back in her chair. Finally, she replied, "Very well, but I must insist that you conduct your investigation while my husband is home. He would not care for strangers wandering about the house unattended. Can you come back tonight, after eight o'clock? We should be finished with dinner by then and he can escort you about the place himself."

Holmes bowed to her condition, "That would be quite satisfactory. If Dr. Watson is available, I should welcome his assistance. I assure you that you will not be double billed for this service."

"Thank you, Dr. Scott. I shall see that all is ready for you."

Her demeanour indicated that our interview was at an end, so we rose, bid her good day and left for Baker Street. I had no rounds that day, my position at St. Bartholomew's hospital being intermittent. Therefore, Holmes and I sat down to enjoy tea and biscuits prepared by Mrs. Hudson.

"So, 'Dr. Scott'," I began. "What do you think of Mrs. Morgan's situation?"

"I found her very interesting, Watson. Tell me her symptoms again, when you first examined her."

"Abdominal pain, fever and skin irritation." I recounted. "She also exhibited diarrhoea while in hospital, but that was gone by the end of the first day."

"What sort of skin irritation?"

"An irregular patch of redness, roughly seven inches in diameter, on the right side of her abdomen."

"No blisters or warts?"

"Not yet."

Holmes proceeded to fill and light his old briarwood pipe and settled back in thought. After several minutes in this posture, while I read the morning paper, he finally spoke, "I believe I shall take a visit to the London Library, then drop across the street to the East India Club as well."

"Is there anything I can do, Holmes?"

"I shall need your assistance in distracting members of the household during my searches this evening, Doctor. You may contemplate some plausible excuses to keep them engaged."

With that odd request, he was out the door and gone for most of the afternoon. He returned just after five o'clock with a look upon his face which I could not quite comprehend. "Did you discover something significant, Holmes?" I asked.

"Consider, Watson," he stated, as he removed his outdoor garments and flopped into his chair to light a cigarette, "We have a household with a wealthy middle-aged husband, who deals with Oriental goods and spices. By all accounts he is an honest man, but his success has sparked jealousies among his competitors. He is married to a woman young enough to be his daughter, there is unfortunate prejudice against the marriage in some narrow minded circles, and she is much resented by his son. I verified these facts while I was at the East India Club. She has a servant, whom she claims is of unwavering loyalty. This fact I must observe for myself, but do you agree to this likely scenario so far?"

"That seems to align with what I have observed and been told," I concurred.

"Therefore, we have much data to still gather, Doctor," he declared. "With just these few pieces to the puzzle, I can surmise more than a half dozen theories to explain her situation."

"Oh, come now, Holmes!" I scoffed. "Six possibilities? Surely not!"

"Watson, you are a good and gentle soul," he sighed, with what seemed to be genuine concern. "I can only hope that your exposure to my world does not scar you. But, in my occupation, I am forced to consider the darker sides of every person and the unlikely, but still possible, circumstances of every event or contingency. Allow me to elucidate.

"First, the benign possibility that she has merely been exposed to spoiled food, germs, bacteria, mould spores or some other aspect of her environs. Second, her stepson despises her and has poisoned her. Third, her maidservant secretly resents her and wants to go back to India, which would be a likely result if her mistress dies. Fourth, the butler resents what he perceives as a foreign influence in this once proud and noble house."

"The butler, Holmes?" I interrupted. "That seems far-fetched."

"You would be surprised, Watson, at how deeply some long-standing servants will go to protect the family honour. I am aware of at least one case where the major-domo arranged an 'accident' for the heir apparent because of his shameful public reputation. That act allowed the more suitable younger son to ascend.

"But allow me to continue. Fifth, Mr. Morgan himself. Perhaps he has found the whims of his lustful decision to no longer outweigh the demands or personality of a younger wife of a different culture. Likely he did not realise how much resentment he would incur among his peers in marrying outside his race and now regrets his rashness. Sixth, Anti-Indian radicals, concerned over the spread of Oriental religions by high placed immigrants, have succeeded in infecting her in some fashion.

"I could go on, Watson, but that would be a futile exercise. After we gather more facts tonight, we should be able to narrow the field considerably."

Having finished his discourse, he sat back and casually blew smoke rings into the air. I shook my head slowly and rose to pour myself a brandy at the sideboard. Then I resumed my seat and contemplated my role in what would certainly be an interesting evening.

Chapter Three

Our cab delivered us to Piccadilly at precisely seven forty-five, in spite of Mrs. Morgan's request to arrive after eight o'clock. I questioned my friend as to his disregard for etiquette.

"When dealing with suspects, Watson, one must use any means to keep them off balance. If the entire household is expecting us at eight o'clock, their demeanour will be building in anticipation of that event. Mentally, they are fifteen minutes from being fully prepared. For the innocent this will merely be inconvenient, but adaptable. For the guilty, depending on their personal discipline, it could fluster them into a mistake."

He rang the bell as I nodded, but I still asked, "Wouldn't they have made their preparations as early as possible? Surely they would not wait until the last minute to hide or destroy evidence."

His answer was curtailed by the opening of the door by Dugan, who seemed to take our early arrival in his stride. "Dr. Scott, Dr. Watson. Come in gentlemen. The family is still at dinner, but you may wait in the parlour while I announce you."

"Thank you, Dugan," said Holmes. "We apologize for our early arrival, but our previous meeting at the hospital ended sooner than expected. We certainly don't wish to curtail the family meal. If you would be so kind, would you ask permission for us to begin our examination of the kitchen until it is convenient for Mr. Morgan to join us?"

"Very good, sir," he stated as he took our hats and coats. He left us standing by the parlour fire. The moment he was out the door, Holmes bid me to play lookout while he made a quick surveillance of the room. In the space of less than two minutes, he noted wear patterns in the carpet, dust levels on the bookshelves and even the location of a safe behind one painting, before I signalled that Dugan was returning. The butler found his visitors standing where he left us, warming our hands by the fire.

Dugan was not alone, however. Young Whitaker was with him and addressed us as soon as he entered, "Doctors, I am Whitaker Morgan. My father has asked that I escort you during your examination of the house. I understand you wish to begin in the kitchen?"

His tone was polite and showed no hint of exasperation or annoyance at our presence. He was a fine figure of a lad. Athletic build, clean-shaven with brown wavy hair, roughly five foot ten. His handshake as we introduced ourselves was firm and self-assured. Holmes actually took his hand and turned it palm up in examination, much to our host's surprise. "What is it, Dr. Scott?"

"May I see your left hand as well, Mr. Morgan?" said Holmes. The lad held it up and Holmes clicked his tongue and pronounced, "You are a golfer, I perceive. I could recommend something for your callouses, if you wish."

Whitaker smiled as Holmes let go of his hands, "No need, Doctor. With the warmer weather approaching, I'll be playing often enough to toughen them up against blistering. But how did you know it was golf and not cricket, or some similar sport?"

Holmes smiled and raised his forefinger as if in lecture, "The single-handed sports, such as polo or tennis were eliminated by the presence of wear on both your hands. Cricket would be less likely to cause such extensive damage, as you would take far fewer swings and of much lesser force. This pattern is much more common among golfers."

"Well done, sir," admitted the Morgan heir. "I hope such powers of observation will allow you to put an end to Miss Patel's misery, for my father's sake and the peace of the household. Come, I'll show you to the kitchen."

As we walked, I asked him about the use of his stepmother's maiden name. "If I am not being too indelicate, Mr. Morgan, may I ask why you referred to your stepmother as *Miss Patel*?" We entered the kitchen and Holmes began his search. I hoped this distraction was something he could use. Morgan turned to me with his back toward Holmes and replied, "I was not present at the so-called 'wedding', which I understand was performed under her religion and not my father's. Nor have I seen any British government document legitimizing their union under English law. And she will certainly *never* replace my mother!"

His last word was said with a vehemence hinting at a hidden temper beneath the gentlemanly manners he had exhibited thus far. I nodded in understanding and what I hoped he would assume was silent agreement. All the better to encourage his confidence.

In reply I merely stated, "The actions of middle-aged men are often ... questionable."

"Damned foolhardy, if you'll pardon my language, sir. I love the man, but this decision was absolutely intolerable. I moved out of the house upon his return and only come by for dinner two or three times a week, just to make sure he is healthy and that business goes well."

"You fear for his health?" I asked, somewhat surprised.

"Not to put too fine a point on it, Doctor Watson, but I can only see one reason for him to marry her. Whereas there are several hundred thousand reasons for her to marry him."

Somewhere in the house a clock was striking eight and a young Indian woman came in with a trolley, piled with dirty dishes from the evening meal. Master Morgan called out at her arrival and said, "Doctors, please meet Bala, Miss Patel's maidservant and cook. Bala, this is Dr. Scott and Dr. Watson. They are here to try and find out what is making your mistress ill."

The young woman was dark, much more so than Mrs. Morgan, and appeared slightly younger. Her black hair was tied up behind her head to keep it out of the way as she worked. From its volume I imagined it would be quite long when let down. She was on the stout side, though not obese, and was about five feet tall. When she spoke, it was very proper English, with a deference in her voice that bordered on fear, I thought.

"Good evening, doctors. I pray you will be successful. May I assist you?"

Having finished examining the cupboards, Holmes was about to enter the pantry, but stopped and smiled at the young woman. "Yes, Miss Bala. Could you show us the steps you took to make dinner the other night? The meal before she went to hospital."

"Certainly. Did you wish me to actually prepare it?" she asked.

Holmes smiled at her cooperativeness and replied, "No, that will not be necessary. I would just like to see where you took all the ingredients from and examine the containers themselves."

She took us through the process and Holmes whispered to me to note the combinations, as my army service had taken me into that realm and made me more familiar with Indian cuisine. I only questioned her on one particular item, but she explained that her mistress preferred her food less spicy than normal and this herb would reduce the harshness of some of the traditional ingredients.

Holmes followed her about like a hound on a scent, examining each box, can and jar. In the pantry he also noted the position of every item and its neighbours. In addition, he took a mental inventory of the contents of the larder and examined the air vent and floor as well.

Bala was thorough in her explanations and Holmes asked one more question, "Does your mistress ever assist you, or come in to check on you while you are preparing the meals?"

Bala nodded, "Yes, quite often, though not every time."

Holmes thanked her for her cooperation, then suggested an examination of the bedroom ventilation and windows. Whitaker led us upstairs and into a bedroom with a single bed, but several chests of drawers, a large wardrobe and a rocking chair with a reading lamp.

"Certainly, this is not the master bedroom," I commented.

"No, Dr. Watson, that door over there leads to my father's bedroom. He is a prodigious snorer and both my mother and Miss Patel have used this room in order to be able to sleep. It used to be my nursery."

"Where is your room now?" asked Holmes.

"It's the next one across, though I've moved most of my things out since I rarely spend the night here any more."

"I see," answered Holmes as he looked about the room. "I notice there is a connecting air vent. Just to be safe we should examine your room as well."

Whitaker shrugged his shoulders, "Anything that will put this silliness behind us. I don't know how father puts up with her constant whining."

Holmes tilted his head non-committally and began an examination of the former nursery, checking the ventilation grille, opening the window, inspecting the bedding, carpets and the wardrobes, looking for any sign of mould or infestation. We followed the same procedure in the master bedroom and finally we came to Whitaker's old room. In this room Holmes again opened the window and examined the sill with his magnifying glass, as he had the others. Looking out he noted, "This room is directly above the kitchen, I see."

Whitaker smiled, "Yes, Dr. Scott, a distinct advantage when I was growing up and when mother on occasion would decide to bake some fresh bread or sweetmeats."

Holmes nodded, then proceeded to the open wardrobe where, to our surprise, a tabby cat lay curled up on a blanket on the bottom shelf. It snapped its head up at our approach, then stretched languidly and walked out to rub against Morgan's leg. He knelt and picked the creature up, who responded by nuzzling the young man's jaw.

"This is Marmalade," he said by way of explanation. "She's the one thing I miss about this house. She slept curled at my feet, or up against my stomach during the night and always jumped in my lap any time I tried to read. Her brother, King George, is a grey tabby and usually roams the kitchen and dining room when he's not curled by the fire in the parlour. But this one likes hiding in closets and under beds."

He nuzzled the feline and set it back down. Holmes asked, "Are they good mousers?"

"King George is quite the hunter. I don't believe we've had any sort of creature stirring downstairs, at least not for long, since he took up his post. Marmalade usually stays up here and I've never seen a mouse, dead or alive, on this floor."

"That bodes well for that aspect of any disease," replied Holmes as he looked back into the wardrobe. Then he said to me, "Dr. Watson, would you hand me your medical bag, please?"

I had been carrying it throughout our excursion and obediently handed it over to him. Thinking he may have found something significant, I again engaged Morgan in conversation.

"So, have you ever accompanied your father on any of his trips to the Orient?"

"Once, when I was sixteen. Mother and I both travelled with him," answered the young man. "I remember that it was a long and arduous trip. Mother and I were seasick for much of the voyage. After getting our land legs back again, we did enjoy many of the sights and certainly the warm weather compared to the winter we had left behind in London. But once was enough. I wouldn't care to make that trip again."

I agreed with him and went on to tell him of my service in Afghanistan, which he found quite interesting. By the time I had completed my tale of escape from the Battle at Maiwand, Holmes had finished and declared that he had enough information to test some theories regarding the maladies reported by the mistress of the house. Whitaker led us downstairs and to the parlour, where his father and my patient were waiting, along with King George curled up by the fire.

He left us there to find Dugan to retrieve our hats and coats. Bertram Morgan introduced himself and shook our hands. "Well, Doctors, did you find anything that may be causing Dinah's symptoms?"

Holmes took the lead and replied, "The ingredients in the kitchen and the pots, pans and utensils all seem in order. There is a little mould on the pantry floor, apparently seeping in from outside. Similarly, I discovered some on an upstairs windowsill and in Master Whitaker's wardrobe along the floor of the exterior wall, but none in either of the other two rooms. I was happy to see that the poisons were stored away from any foodstuffs and the mousetraps were all clean. That's probably thanks to this fine fellow," He nodded toward the cat.

Continuing, he said, "I took some samples which I will test in our laboratory. In the meantime, Mrs. Morgan, I suggest you keep to the diet which Dr. Watson has recommended for the time being and report any new symptoms immediately."

We took our leave when Dugan arrived with our coats. As we walked out to the pavement, we were followed by Whitaker, who was also leaving for the evening. We allowed him to take the first cab and I noted that Holmes took special notice of the address given. Then we hailed a cab for Baker Street. As we rode along, I asked my friend, "Well, did you learn anything, Holmes? Have you narrowed your half dozen theories down to a manageable number?"

In reply he tapped my medical bag and said, "I have a strong suspect now, Watson. It all depends on the test results of what is in here."

"So, it is deliberate then? Who's doing it? Whitaker?" I asked.

"All in good time, Watson. We must wait for *Dr. Scott's* test results."

Chapter Four

Once again in our rooms, Holmes retrieved the few samples he had secreted in my bag, two of which, I was surprised to see, were small phials of white powder. These he carefully took out and placed on his makeshift laboratory table.

"Where did those come from, Holmes," I asked. "The pantry?"

"A moment please, Watson," he answered. Holmes then placed some of the powder from one phial in a beaker and added some other chemicals to it to observe the reaction. Then he did the same with powder from the other, which reacted less violently than the first. At last he spoke, "One from Arsenic in the pantry and one from a box labelled 'Arsenic' in Whitaker's wardrobe next to a mousetrap."

"I see," I said. Then after a moment corrected myself, "Actually, I don't see. What is the significance of that?"

He interlocked his fingers and, with his elbows on the table, held his hands under his chin in thought as he replied, "It is not uncommon to cover the bait in mousetraps with arsenic or some other poison, as the creatures quite often snare the tidbits without getting caught. I found it unusual, however, that the box should be left in the wardrobe of Whitaker's room. Why was it there if a cat is on guard? Why wasn't it put away? And why is this particular batch so weak?"

"Do you have a theory?" I queried.

He walked over to the mantelpiece and stuffed his old clay pipe with tobacco from the Persian slipper which hung there. Lighting it, he settled into his basket chair and finally replied, "I must smoke a pipe or two on it, Watson. My findings point toward a theory that seems too fantastic, but still may be the truth and I need to consider all the factors at hand before pursuing it. I beg you not to speak to me for at least one hour."

I poured myself a brandy and settled down with a cigar and an evening paper, turning the pages as quietly as possible, so as not to disturb my friend. Finally, he rushed to the door, throwing on his homburg and overcoat. "I'm going out for a bit, Watson. I shouldn't be long, but don't wait up."

I've seen him make these abrupt exits before and have come to accept them as a quirk of his personality. At least this time he acknowledged my presence before departing. As it was now close to eleven o'clock, I decided to take myself off to bed in preparation for early morning rounds at Bart's the next day. As I drifted off to sleep, all the possibilities Holmes had enumerated circled about my brain and I attempted to use my observations of the evening to pin down the proper explanation, but sleep came long before an answer.

The next morning, I arose and found Holmes at the breakfast table, ignoring Mrs. Hudson's preparations and opting for just tea. As I sat with him, I picked out some bacon and wrapped it between two slices of warm bread. I also poured myself some tea, before finally enquiring, "How did your evening excursion go, Holmes?"

"It was satisfactory, Doctor. I've enlisted an ally in our quest, but I also need to conduct more research at the hospital library. Would you mind sharing a cab this morning?"

"Certainly not, Holmes, you're most welcome. Is there anything that I might be able to answer for you?"

He shook his head slowly, "If my suspicions are correct, the question itself would be beyond the comprehension of most medical men and would likely not be something they could answer without conducting the same research which I shall perform this morning. Thank you, Doctor, but I would rather not expose you to the dark recesses of the diabolical plot I fear, until I am sure of all the facts."

Arriving at the hospital, we went our separate ways. After about two hours, I ran into him again. Without breaking stride, he merely said, "Pieces are falling into place, Watson. I now have a desire for a meal which reflects our case, which I believe shall be best served at the East India Club. I shall meet you back at Baker Street when you have attended to the patients at your practice."

The rest of my day, however, was anything but routine. Just after lunch, Mrs. Morgan, accompanied by Bala, was again brought into an examination room. Her symptoms were the same as previously, though not quite as severe. During my questioning, it occurred to me to ask, "The last time you came in, you said your husband ate the same food as you, but Master Whitaker had a more traditional English meal. Did the same thing occur last night?"

Sensing her mistresses' distress, Bala answered instead, "Yes, Dr. Watson, sir. He came to the kitchen while I was preparing dinner and picked out his own food for me to cook. The same thing happened the other night."

"I see," I said, nodding in thought. "Your husband is feeling no ill effects this time either?"

Clenching her stomach, my patient answered through gritted teeth, "No, he's fine!"

I decided to admit her again overnight with a prescription to address her discomfort. As I pondered her situation and considered what I had learned the previous night, it seemed too coincidental that her attacks occurred each time that Whitaker joined them for dinner. Bala's statement that he had been in the kitchen also supported the possibility of an opportunity for him to administer the poison. Though I did wonder why the poison in his room was weaker than that found in the kitchen. Was he only trying to make her sick without killing her? Was he building up a case of long-term exposure that would eventually lead to her demise? Even with his obvious dislike of her, I found it incongruous that the young man I met last night could devise so deadly a plot.

33

Yet, by the time I met up with my companion back at Baker Street, I was convinced that this was the most likely scenario. I expressed my concerns to Holmes as we sat by the fire.

"Watson, dear fellow, I daresay you have put together a circumstantial case and have not allowed your personal judgement of the man's cordial personality to cloud your judgement of what seem to be incontrovertible facts. For that, I congratulate you."

I found myself momentarily pleased at his acknowledgement of my summation. Then he spoke again.

"You are, however, not in possession of all the facts which I gleaned last night and have leapt to an erroneous conclusion. I take full responsibility for this, in that I did not share everything I learned with you, a habit I developed long ago, I'm afraid."

My countenance fell, momentarily, but rebounded when I realized this meant that young Whitaker was innocent. "Well, who is the culprit, Holmes?" I countered.

Instead of answering immediately, he asked a question of his own, "When do you expect to release Mrs. Morgan from hospital this time, Doctor?"

I pursed my lips in thought and replied, "Her symptoms are not quite so severe this time. I imagine she'll be out by tomorrow afternoon. Why?"

Holmes consulted a calendar and finally replied, "Then I believe that we shall have our answer this coming Sunday. I have arrangements to make, but that can be done in the morning. I do need you to do one thing for me, Doctor."

He made his request and I protested that such an action would be completely unethical, but he calmed me and stated, "I assure you, Watson, you will not be performing such a procedure, I just need Mrs. Morgan to believe that you will, so she will take that news to her household when she returns home.

"Very well, Holmes," I agreed, reluctantly. "I hope you know what you're doing."

"Always a method to my madness, old friend. For tonight, I suggest a quiet evening enjoying Mrs. Hudson's roast chicken and a good book."

Chapter Five

By Sunday evening Mrs. Morgan was home again, having been discharged from the hospital three days earlier. Holmes left me at Baker Street at about five o'clock with instructions that I should engage a cab and have the driver take me to the Morgan home and wait outside at precisely seven o'clock. I would be joined there at that time by Inspector Lestrade of Scotland Yard. At shortly after seven, Holmes would come out and retrieve us.

I arrived as scheduled and was soon joined by the weasel-faced Inspector, who peppered me with questions. "Do you know what he's up to, Dr. Watson? He'd better pray he's not wasting my time on a Sunday evening. I get little enough time off work. All he told me was that he needed me to make an arrest."

I advised the Scotland Yarder of the situation and that Holmes expected to unmask a potential murderer before the deed was done. I also had to admit I did not know precisely who the culprit was, only that it was likely to be a member of the household.

Lestrade sniffed in displeasure, "Your friend always plays his cards close to his chest. Someday that will cause him more trouble than he can handle."

I attempted to placate Lestrade by offering him a cigarette, but he politely declined and we waited in silence. At about ten minutes past the hour, the butler, Dugan, came out of the house and approached our cab. Seeing me, he announced, "Dr. Watson, your colleague has just revealed that he is really Sherlock Holmes, some sort of detective. He requested your presence in the dining room. Is this the police inspector?"

"Yes," I replied. "This is Inspector Lestrade of Scotland Yard."

"Very good, sir. His presence is requested as well. If you will follow me?"

The scene was one of dismay and agitation. Bertram Morgan was sitting at his place at the head of the dining table. His plate pushed away and food untouched. The look on his face was one of disbelief and shock. Whitaker was standing to the side of the fireplace, fists clenched and face red in anger. Holmes was between the fireplace and the dining table, standing with arms folded and maintaining his calm yet firm disposition. Directly in front of the fire was Mrs. Morgan, looking hot with rage and holding a poker like a cricket bat, as if to stave away any attempt to subdue her. Her eyes flashed from Holmes to Whitaker until she saw us.

"Dr. Watson!" she shouted. "Tell this fool he is insane!"

Lestrade took the lead and stepped forward. "All right then, Mr. Holmes, would you care to explain what's going on? Just who am I here to arrest?"

Before Holmes could reply, the lady of the house pointed at Whitaker and screamed, "Him! He's been trying to kill me! He keeps poisoning my food!"

"Calm down, madam," ordered the Inspector. "I'll take all your statements, but first I want Mr. Holmes' explanation."

Knowing that Whitaker was on guard against any movement by his father's wife, Holmes strode over to stand between us and the senior Morgan, still sitting in shock, and began his case.

"When Dr. Watson came to me with his suspicions of the lady being poisoned, I agreed to look into the matter. Certainly, Master Whitaker had reason to be rid of his stepmother, but after observing the man, examining the house and conducting discreet investigations at the East India Club, I was fairly convinced of his innocence.

"But there were troubling issues here in the house itself. Most notably, when I found a box of arsenic in Whitaker's old room, where it did not logically belong."

"See!" cried Mrs. Morgan. "That proves it! He's been the one poisoning me!"

Holmes gave her a look and Whitaker took a step toward her, causing her to raise the poker even higher. She fell silent and the detective continued his report.

"I determined that the box had been planted there, next to the mousetrap so it would appear it was just forgotten. I deduced that the son would not do so, as he was aware that the cat, Marmalade was a sufficient deterrent against rodents in that part of the house. However, as with many containers of powdery substances, having been opened and used, there was a slight residue on the outside of the box. Perfect for retaining finger marks. My examination revealed that the marks left behind on this box were far too small to be those of Whitaker Morgan. They were more the size of a woman. The only other woman in the house is Bala, the maidservant and cook. She, however, is of a stout nature with much shorter and fatter fingers than the impressions I found. That left Mrs. Morgan.

"Chemical tests of the arsenic in that box compared to arsenic taken from the box in the pantry, revealed a much weaker strain. One which would cause illness, but not necessarily death, especially to one who had been exposed to arsenic poisoning in her childhood in India."

He looked pointedly at the lady and she lowered the poker and brought her fist to her mouth, where she nervously began biting her hand in fear of being exposed.

"That information I gained through associates at the East India Club, where I also heard rumours of her having a young suitor, before she was married off to Mr. Morgan as part of a business deal."

Now the lady sank to the floor and buried her head in her hands, clearly undone.

I spoke up and asked the obvious, "Do you mean to say she was poisoning herself, Holmes? To what end?"

"Her mind has a devious bent, Doctor. Just as in the boxing ring, where I feign injuries to lure my opponents in, then strike at the opportune time, she made it *appear* as if she were the intended victim. In reality, she planned on using the fatal act as a botched attempt on her life that went awry. She would frame the son for the murder of his father as an attack that was meant for her. Bertram would be dead. Whitaker would be sentenced to either death or life imprisonment and she would be free to use the Morgan fortune as she chose, likely to return to India where her true love was waiting."

Lestrade then asked, "Obviously the man is still sitting here quite alive, Holmes. Where is your proof?"

"If you will confiscate Mr. Morgan's dinner plate, you will have all the proof you need, for it contains a high concentration of arsenic, hidden by the mixture of spices. In addition, I witnessed her place the poison in the food myself."

"Impossible!" she shouted, in one last attempt at pleading her innocence.

Holmes turned to me, "Doctor, you recall my saying that I had enlisted an ally to our cause?"

"Yes, you told me that the other day, but didn't say who."

He pointed to Whitaker, "Our friend here was more than eager to help, once I explained my suspicions. He drilled a hole in his wardrobe floor between the rafters and into the kitchen ceiling above the counter where the food is prepared. He was able to accomplish this on Saturday morning before you discharged your patient. Bala was out, his father at work, and Dugan was quite willing to assist. I merely had to move an old pair of shoes and I could see directly into the kitchen. He let me in through the back door well before dinner and I was clearly able to watch her add the arsenic from the full-strength box to her husband's meal while Bala's back was turned"

A groan came up from Bertram and I feared he might faint, so I went to his side and handed him his wine glass, first ascertaining from Holmes that it was not poisoned. Then I asked, "How did you know she would administer the fatal dose tonight?"

"The power of suggestion and manipulation of circumstances, Watson. When I asked you to tell her that if another bout of illness occurred you would need to perform exploratory surgery, it pressed her to action. She could not credibly pull off another weakened attack on herself, so she would have to charge forward with her final move. Of course, it had to be on a night when Whitaker was invited to dinner, so she would have her Judas to blame. I suggested to him to make it known that he was leaving for a three-month trip to the Continent on business. That set the stage for him to come this evening for a final meal and she, fearing this would be her last chance for months, fell into the trap."

Lestrade stepped forward, took the poker from Mrs. Morgan's hand and pulled her up from the floor. "Dinah Morgan, I hereby arrest you for the attempted murder of Bertram Morgan. Anything you say will be taken down and used against you. Time to come with me."

He handcuffed her behind her back and led her out of the house to the police van that had been waiting since he had joined me in my cab. Holmes and I followed with the poisoned dinner plate in a box provided by Dugan. With his prisoner and evidence in hand, the Inspector bid us a good evening and directed the driver back to Scotland Yard.

We returned to the house to offer our condolences to the Morgan men. We found the father embracing his son and apologizing profusely. Seeing us, he released Whitaker and came over to shake our hands, taking special effort with my companion.

"Mr. Holmes, I am in your debt. You saved my life and my son. Whatever fee you deem appropriate, please send me your bill."

We took our leave and returned to Baker Street where we sat with our evening brandies in front of a fire. Holmes took out his index book and made a few notes. I also jotted down the facts he had revealed that evening, which I have recorded here. It struck me as amusing that here were a former army surgeon and an up and coming detective, both under the age of thirty, sitting like a couple of old college professors making notes for a lecture. I raised my glass in Holmes' direction and declared, "To you, Mr. Sherlock Holmes, congratulations on solving a most singular case!"

My friend acknowledged my praise with his own raised glass, "Thank you, Watson, but really, once I had all the facts, it was quite elementary."

*****

"My collection of M's is a fine one," said he. *"Moriarty himself is enough to make any letter illustrious, and here is Morgan the poisoner …."* Sherlock Holmes to Dr. Watson in *The Empty House* by Arthur Conan Doyle.

The Dead Quiet Library

Chapter One

In early May of 1895, not long after our cycling adventure with Miss Violet Smith[1] and her notorious suitors, my friend, the consulting detective Sherlock Holmes, and I were enjoying a leisurely lunch. I was pouring myself a second cup of tea when we heard the doorbell ring and, soon after, the distinctive tread of footsteps ascending to our rooms.

"A case, Watson," declared Holmes. "Unless I'm much mistaken, for surely I hear young Stanley Hopkins approaching."

No sooner had the words left him than we faced the recently promoted Scotland Yard Inspector. Nearly thirty years of age, Hopkins reminded me a little of Holmes, tall and lean, with a thin face. Like me, however, he sported a moustache, which almost gave him a military air.

Climbing the seventeen steps to our rooms was certainly no great effort for a fit young man. Yet there was a pained expression on his face, like that of a troubled soul. I insisted he sit immediately. I motioned him to the chair where I knew Holmes preferred to observe his potential clients and poured him a cup of tea.

Holmes left the dining table and sat across from our visitor. He leaned back in that casual posture of his, meant to put guests at ease, and spoke in a conversational tone.

---

[1] *The Solitary Cyclist* -Arthur Conan Doyle

"Good afternoon, Inspector. What troubles have the citizens of Chadwell Heath laid at your feet on this fine spring day?"

"How do you do that, Mr. Holmes? Yes, I was called out to St. Chad's College first thing this morning."

"There are burrs of a plant which is prominent in St. Chad's Park attached to your trouser cuffs and a train ticket stub in your hatband is quite obvious," answered the detective. "Has another mysterious death intruded upon that bucolic institution?"

"I see you are aware of the incident which occurred two months ago," responded Hopkins. "It was ruled accidental, but the circumstances have left a shadow of doubt among those of us at the Yard. Now a second death has occurred and I'm not so sure we don't have a calculating murderer on our hands, Mr. Holmes."

Being unfamiliar with the previous incident, I queried Hopkins. "I had not heard of any mysterious deaths out in Chadwell Heath, Inspector. What has aroused your suspicion?"

Holmes chimed in, "Yes, Hopkins, please refresh our memory and I beg you, tell us all and not just what the newspapers reported."

The young man set down his teacup and leaned back to settle himself as he began his tale. "Two months ago, on Friday, the eighth of March, a student named Aloysius Bass was in the Lansbury Library at St. Chad's. His reasons for being there were never confirmed. He was not a studious sort and there were rumours about his assignations with young ladies. As you should be aware, St. Chad's has followed the example of University College, Bristol[1] and admits women to its student population. At any rate, somehow, he remained in the building after the nine o'clock closing. Avoiding the librarian would not have been difficult if it was intentional, for it was assumed that

---

[1] University College, Bristol was one of the first higher education colleges in England to allow mixed education for men and women – the first being the University of London in 1869.

all visitors would wish to be reminded of how late it was and leave voluntarily when the closing bell was sounded.

"The next morning, being a Saturday, the library did not open until ten o'clock. The librarian, one Orson O'Hare, is an elderly gentleman. With his bifocal glasses, however, his vision is quite normal, though his hearing is weak in one ear. His mind is sharp and memory superb. When he opened the doors for the day, he took up his post at the front desk and waited on visiting students and professors as usual. It wasn't until around ten forty-five that someone had occasion to visit the third floor, which is the uppermost of the building, and found the body of Mr. Bass."

"Good Lord!" I exclaimed.

Holmes added, "As I recall it was reported that he died of a broken neck. Did the police surgeon pinpoint a time of death?"

Hopkins continued, "He believed it to be between nine and ten o'clock the previous evening. He was found at the base of a book ladder and a volume from the top shelf was on the floor next to him, so it was believed he simply slipped and fell."

"But you are not convinced it was accidental," stated Holmes.

"Even the coroner was reluctant to state so," replied Hopkins. "But there was no conclusive evidence to the contrary, so it was ruled a 'Death by Misadventure'."

"Pray tell us, what was nagging at your mind back then?"

"As I said, Bass was not the studious type. His being there on a Friday night was totally out of character, so what was the reason? Also, the break to his neck. It was not a snapping, horizontal break as one might assume from landing on his head. It was a violent twist that one would expect from a human agent, especially if they had military training. Finally, there's the reputation of the library itself."

"Reputation?" I queried. "What do you mean, Inspector?"

He shifted uncomfortably and leaned forward with his elbows on his knees. "The library was once the ancestral home of Sir Osbert Lansbury, and legend has it that he still haunts the place."

"Poppycock!" declared Holmes in disgust at such a suggestion.

"And this relates to your case in some way?" I asked, attempting to be more sympathetic to Hopkins' predicament.

"Not that I believe in ghosts, Doctor," he said. "However, there have been occasional sightings of a cloaked figure and unusual sounds heard, in what otherwise is an extremely quiet building due to its thick walls and heavy doors. Now that there has been a second suspicious death, I cannot merely dismiss such evidence out of hand."

"Tell us about this new victim and the circumstances of his demise," asked Holmes, impatiently.

Hopkins leaned back again and took a notepad from his breast pocket, referring to it as he reported. "Clifton Douglas, age forty-two, athletics and rugby coach. Married, no children. Has been in his position for eleven years. Found in the library this morning, again on the third floor. The police surgeon puts time of death at roughly between nine and ten last night, just like Bass. This time, however, the cause of death appears to be a trip and fall. There was a rug rumpled at his feet and a gash along his left temple as he apparently tripped and hit his head on the corner of a reading table."

The young Inspector snapped his notebook shut and put it into his pocket saying, "I don't like it one bit, Mr. Holmes. Two violent accidents resulting in death this close together in such a peaceful location are much too coincidental for me. Also, whether it means anything or not, Bass was a fullback on Douglas' rugby team. One of his star players, in fact."

Holmes leaned back and steepled his fingers, head toward the ceiling but eyes closed in thought. He held this position for nearly a minute. I could see Hopkins' patience wearing thin. Just as the Inspector opened his mouth to speak, Holmes jumped up suddenly and said, "We must go to Chadwell Heath immediately! I presume the police surgeon has the body?"

"Yes, Mr. Holmes," replied Hopkins.

The detective strode over to our writing table and jotted down a quick note. This he dropped at the telegraph office at the railway station. When questioned by the Inspector, he merely stated that he had sent a request to the police surgeon, hoping to preserve evidence until we arrived.

The trip to Chadwell Heath was fairly quick, being a mere twelve miles away with a direct line from Liverpool Street station. The three of us crowded into a cab upon arrival at the red brick station and were in the police surgeon's office shortly after eleven o'clock.

He was a rather young fellow named Dr. Palmer, who greeted us with enthusiasm, "Mr. Holmes, Dr. Watson, a pleasure to meet you, sirs. I hope you can prove to the coroner that we have a killer on our hands."

He led us to the post mortem room and pointed out the latest resident of the examining table. "His death was no accident, just like that of Aloysius Bass. No mere trip and fall would have delivered sufficient force to cause this head wound and death."

Holmes questioned the young man, "If you are sure of Bass' cause of death, why did it get reported as an accident?"

Palmer leaned in conspiratorially and spoke softly, "The coroner, Robert Caldwell, is an alumnus of St. Chad's and is adamant about avoiding adverse publicity. The old stories of the haunted library had faded into ancient history and he wants nothing stirred up that would affect future enrolment. It's rumoured that the college is suffering financially and any significant reduction in student population could cause it to shut down."

"Surely," I exclaimed, "he cannot condone letting a murderer get away; especially now that he's apparently struck again!"

"There was no proof of a second party in the room the first time," chimed in Hopkins. "With just the twisted neck theory there were no supporting facts for a murder."

Palmer fumed, "It's no *theory*, Inspector. No matter how he landed from that fall off the ladder, (if he even fell), hitting his head on the floor would not have resulted in that twisting break of his vertebrae. There was also just a light bump above his left ear and no other bruising. How did he hit his head hard enough to break his neck without leaving a more significant mark? No, sir! Bass was murdered, and I'll wager that this fellow was, too."

Holmes stared down at the body of Clifton Douglas, but instead of taking a closer look, made a request of Dr. Palmer. "I'd like to examine his clothes. Where are they?"

Palmer led us over to a nearby shelf and pulled out a box that he set on a table. Hopkins and I observed as Holmes methodically went through Douglas' clothing, paying special attention to his coat and shirt. He also gave a cursory look at the soles of his shoes before returning all the items to the box.

"There is certainly nothing about his shoes that would explain a misstep or trip," began Holmes. "However, he is missing the second button from his shirt and the shirt itself is quite wrinkled at that point. Almost as if someone had grabbed it in their fist."

He gave a telling look to Hopkins as he made this statement and then took a closer look at the body. Magnifying lens in hand, my old friend made minute observations of the victim's hand, even going so far as to borrow some tweezers to extract something from beneath the fingernails. He then proceeded to examine the legs, feet, chest, back, arms and finally the head wound itself.

When he finished, Palmer spoke without even waiting for Holmes' conclusion. "I'm right, aren't I, Mr. Holmes?" It was more statement than question. The tall detective leaned back against a post, tapping his lens to his lips as he stared down at the lifeless form of the former academic. At last he put his glass back into his pocket and replied, "You are, Dr. Palmer, without a doubt. Gentlemen, we have a murder to solve."

Chapter Two

Y ou're sure, Mr. Holmes?" asked Hopkins. "There's no evidence of anyone else being there."

"We shall take a look for ourselves, Inspector. Douglas here has fibres from some fabric other than the clothes he was wearing under his fingernails, where he likely grabbed his attacker in self-defence. They appear to be from a blue coat or cloak, possibly a sports jacket. There are also hairs pulled from his chest where he was grabbed in the motion that undoubtedly caused his shirt button to be torn off. In addition, there is bruising to the body, arms and legs where he would have been grabbed, punched and kicked in a struggle that ended with his head being slammed against the table top as his feet were swept out from under him."

"Surely someone would have heard such a confrontation, Holmes," I said.

"From the time of death, Watson, it was likely after hours" he replied. "Even if it were right at closing time, a strong, athletic man like Douglas may have been over-confident in his ability against his opponent and chosen not to use energy or break his concentration by crying out. The struggle itself was on the top floor and the noise may have been insufficient to carry to the floors below, especially in a building that has a reputation for being so quiet."

Palmer spoke up, "If it means anything, Mr. Holmes, St. Chad College's biggest rival is Ashlyn College over in Chigwell and their college colour is blue, whereas St. Chad's is green.

Holmes nodded at this information and commanded, "Come gentlemen," as he swept out of the room. "We must examine the scene of the crime before crucial evidence is lost."

We reacquired a cab and made the short trip to St. Chad's and the Lansbury Library in mere minutes. Before we went in, Holmes insisted on investigating the grounds around the outside of the building. The walls were guarded by a thick hedge that could not easily be penetrated. The only break in this greenery was along the windows on the east and west sides of the ground floor. My companion made careful observation of the earth beneath each one and scribbled a note. When he had completed his rounds, we entered the facility and I was struck by the absolute silence, such as I've only experienced at the Diogenes Club.[1]

The reception area included tapestries, coats of arms of the Lansburys and other related families and a suit of armour, labelled as belonging to Sir Osbert Lansbury, himself. I noted it's size and commented, "Sir Osbert wasn't a very large fellow for a knight. This looks like it was made for a chap only about five foot six, perhaps shorter."

"Three hundred years ago that wasn't short, Watson," observed my companion. "The average height of mankind creeps ever upward as healthier foods and lifestyles enable more conducive conditions for growth. You and I are certainly tall for our times, but I imagine that a hundred years from now we would find ourselves merely average."[2]

We proceeded inside and found that, to ensure the quiet, the librarian's desk was enclosed by wood and glass walls so

---

[1] Sherlock Holmes' elder brother Mycroft was a founding member of the Diogenes Club. Speaking is absolutely forbidden, except in the Strangers' Room, where the two brothers would occasionally meet to discuss a case.

[2] Watson describes Holmes as 'rather over six feet' in *A Study in Scarlet* by Arthur Conan Doyle. Based on the Sidney Paget drawings of Holmes and Watson, the Doctor was not much shorter, perhaps five foot ten or eleven.

conversation could be held behind a closed door. Fortunately, it was quite roomy, as it had to accommodate students lining up to check out materials.

Orson O'Hare sat on a tall stool behind a counter as he dealt with students. When he stood to greet us, I judged him to be about five foot eight and a stocky two hundred pounds. His brown hair was parted in the middle and flowed back in waves until it curled over his collar. There were grey streaks along the temples and his short beard and moustache were completely grey with just slight streaks of brown stubbornly showing through. He wore gold-rimmed, bi-focal eyeglasses and spoke in a pleasant baritone voice as he addressed us.

"Hello again, Inspector. Are these the gentlemen you spoke of this morning?"

"Yes, Mr. O'Hare," answered Hopkins. "This is Mr. Sherlock Holmes and Dr. John Watson. I wanted you to meet them before we went upstairs to examine the scene."

"A pleasure, gentlemen," he replied as he shook our hands in turn with a strong grip for a man of his age. "I will be happy to answer any questions you may have, but in the meantime, feel free to look around."

We took our leave and proceeded up the staircase to the top floor. Hopkins had taken the precaution to surround the area where the body had been found with chairs. A handwritten note was fastened to one, stating that the area was to remain undisturbed, so that any students on that floor would not contaminate the scene. Holmes congratulated the young man on his foresight.

Immediately my old friend set to work. He removed the chairs and carefully studied the floor. Except for the rugs under the tables to reduce the noise of chairs being pulled in and out, the flooring was of polished oak planks. The bookshelves, which wound around most of the perimeter included four long, free-standing aisles, took up two thirds of the room. They were likewise of thick oak to support the weight of volumes residing there and stretched all the way to the ten feet high ceiling. Each row had a rolling ladder suspended from the top for students to reach the highest levels. The rest of the room was set up as a study area of six rectangular tables with two chairs on each side.

"Why is this room so large?" I pondered. "You would think this floor would be devoted to bedrooms."

"You're thinking of it as a home, dear Doctor," answered Holmes. While not a castle in the true sense, it was meant to be a fortified structure. This floor was likely an armoury with access to the roof for archers defending against the enemy."

We continued our examination and at one point, Holmes laid down on the floor, positioning himself so the spot where the body fell caught the light of the windows on the west side of the room as it filtered down the long aisles formed by the bookshelves. Then he took up the curled over corner of the rug and laid in flat again. There lay the missing button from Douglas' shirt.

A satisfied 'Aha!' escaped his lips as he rose to his knees. He handed the button to the Inspector and bid him to get down and observe what else he had seen. Hopkins complied, then stood again shaking his head. "I don't know how I could have missed that."

"What is it?" I asked, not deigning to test the limits of my old war wound by attempting to lower and then raise myself from the floor. "Footmarks, Doctor, and not those of Mr. Douglas, answered Holmes. "These have a rubber sole, all the more suitable for sneaking up behind someone. As for missing them, Hopkins," he continued, addressing the young man, "do not fault yourself. Your examination was made this morning, long before the advantage of having the afternoon sun streaming through the windows."

"Then, there *was* a second person here," I said. "very likely the killer."

Holmes stood and brushed off his trouser knees. "A distinct possibility, Doctor. Although, the button could have just fallen off and Douglas tripped attempting to retrieve it. However, given the condition of his shirt I find that unlikely. Unfortunately, there is no way to know for certain when those shoe marks were made. They are fairly fresh, but it's still possible they were made by someone who helped remove the body. Do you have knowledge of who that was, Inspector?"

"Palmer will know the name of the men who assisted him. I'll find out for you Mr. Holmes."

"So," I commented with a wry grin, "you haven't completely eliminated the ghost yet."

Holmes gave me a surly look and replied, "Watson, please. The only ghost here was the departing spirit of Clifton Douglas."

Having finished his examination of the floor, he then began a perimeter search of the room, starting with the windows. The bottom of the sills were about three feet up from the floor and extended six feet up toward the ceiling. There were four of them, each about three feet wide and capable of being opened by sliding the bottom half up. It was quite obvious that these were modern additions to the building, as structures of this style in the late sixteenth century would not have had windows of that type. Holmes checked each one, looking for footmarks on the sill and observing the outside, to determine if anyone could have climbed up from the ground or descended on a rope from the roof. Satisfied that these were not the approach of the killer, he then began inspecting the walls.

Curiosity got the better of Hopkins who asked, "Could not the killer merely have walked in like any other visitor and laid in wait for his victim? Perhaps he lured Douglas here by some message, struck at the opportune moment, then merely walked out with everyone else when the library closed, or even afterward."

Holmes replied over his shoulder as he examined the bookshelves along the wall, "Certainly plausible, but I believe unlikely, Inspector. Our killer would wish to keep his presence in the library unknown, if possible. Especially if someone could connect him with a motive for killing these men. If you noticed the lock on the front door, you would know that once it is locked, no one can get in or out without a key. In his position, I had surmised that Douglas would be one of those entrusted with one and there was a key of that type among his personal belongings at the mortuary. That also confirms that the killer didn't take it, yet he was not afraid of being locked in the building after closing. Therefore, since he did not need Douglas' key to leave, and yet he wished to not be noticed among the visitors going in and out, we have two possibilities."

Hopkins snapped his fingers and exclaimed, "He had a key of his own!"

Holmes gave that brief flash of a smile of his and turned toward the young Scotland Yarder, "A possibility we must explore. While we are here, it is conducive to investigate the only other option available. That the killer has intimate knowledge of this ancient structure and is familiar with some secret passage, which were quite common in those turbulent times."

"Like a priest's hole?" I queried.

"Exactly, Watson. Somewhere in which our culprit could hide out for the night and then slip out at any time the next day when the library was re-opened. Or, more likely, leave by way of a tunnel that exits far away from the building."

Chapter Three

I noticed, as Holmes crept along the wall in search of such an exit, that he concentrated his observation only on two areas. One between three and a half and four feet above the floor and the other along the floorboards. Hopkins also took note and questioned his mentor.

"Why are you concentrating on the wall at that particular height, Holmes? Couldn't a secret locking mechanism be anywhere?"

"I will certainly expand the search parameters if necessary, Inspector. However, I am attempting to save time by observing the two likeliest locations. Somewhere along the base of the wall could be a catch that is operated by one's foot. There is a disadvantage as such a device could be accidentally operated by someone cleaning the floor, but mechanically it is a sound placement. This particular area along the wall," he said, waving his hand in a sideways motion, "is based upon Sir Osbert's height of roughly five foot six inches. There would likely be a manual release somewhere between his waist and chest where he would have the most leverage to operate it.

"May I suggest, gentlemen, that you also pay particular attention to the floor and note any signs of disturbed dust, or scratches from a swinging door. Although I believe it far more likely that such a door will swing into the wall, one cannot discount other directions. You should also keep an eye out for any type of spyhole or movable slot where someone inside the wall could observe the interior of this room before opening the door."

Hopkins and I took these instructions to heart and chose other sections to assist in the search where the walls appeared thick enough to admit human passage. As Holmes neared the corner, I saw him suddenly stop and study an ancient shield on display on the wall between the windows and the bookshelves. It was a ceremonial shield showing no wear nor indentations from use and it was shined to a high silver gloss, obviously a result of the current era cleaning crew. It bore the crest of the Lansburys; a knight's helmet with red plume atop a standard shield with a red rose, yellow lion, brown oak tree and a blue lyre within the four quadrants created by a red cross upon it.

Holmes walked up to it, studiously looking back and forth from it to the perpendicular shelf that formed the corner of the room. Holding his hands up with splayed fingers, he began to study the bookshelf at roughly the height of his own shoulder, which I realized must be about eye level for Sir Osbert.

Suddenly, he reached forth and grasped a vertical support for that particular shelf and manipulated it until it turned about forty-five degrees. The empty space behind aligned perfectly with the shining shield. Peering in with the help of a lit match, one could see the landing where someone could hide. The three of us excitedly examined the edges around the shelving until Holmes found a catch that enabled that section of the bookcase to swivel on a central post. It swung open slowly, ingeniously suspended by the smallest fraction of an inch above the floor, so as to be unnoticeable by anyone standing in front of the shelf.

Within the thick wall was a landing, where one could stand and observe the reflection of the room in that shining shield. There were wall sconces for ancient torches and stone stairs leading downward. The light of the windows with the door opened was sufficient for us to see to the next landing and we descended the steps to the second floor.

There, Holmes found another 'spyhole' and gazed about the room before opening the door. This appeared to be a bedroom that had been converted to a meeting room and was unoccupied. We entered and this floor featured a central open space where the stairwell wound through and a landing wound all the way around it. Then we saw a mannequin of what was ostensibly a likeness of Sir Osbert Lansbury in court dress. This turned out to be on a wheeled platform along the east wall, facing toward the campus. Holmes took a quick glance around and seemed to take great interest in Sir Osbert's attire. Then he ordered us back into the passage where we came to another landing. This looked out upon the first floor but Holmes was on the scent. By now we had descended beyond the daylight from our original ingress and Holmes pulled a candle from his coat.

Hopkins declared, "How did you happen to have a candle with you, Holmes? I swear, sometimes watching you work seems like witchcraft!"

The detective responded over his shoulder as he continued to lead the way, "I anticipated a secret passage, given the scene of the crime, Inspector. Had we not been informed of this location, it's likely we would be attempting this descent by the light of whatever materials were at hand, if any were available. Watch your step!"

That warning came as the stone step beneath his feet rocked from imbalance at the loss of ancient mortar. We navigated it safely and stopped briefly at the ground floor. Again, Holmes peeped out to note our location, which was at the rear of a pantry that was part of the kitchen. He slid a panel aside and found a paraffin lantern on a nearby shelf. He inspected it briefly. It was about half full and in working order. He extinguished his candle, lit the mantle of the lantern and we continued our descent as the secret passage steps continued downward.

"As I suspected, there is an underground tunnel trailing off to the west. Look here, Hopkins. There are traces of fresh footprints and the cobwebs have been swept away. This tunnel has seen recent use, no doubt. Let us see where it leads."

The Inspector hesitated and I noted some physical symptoms which concerned me. "Are you all right, Hopkins?"

I enquired. Holmes looked back and spoke before the young man answered. "It may not be wise for the three of us to journey forth, since no one knows where we are. You should remain here, Inspector and keep an ear out for any sounds of distress, should the tunnel prove unstable. We will return shortly. Here, take the candle for yourself."

I could see a visible wave of relief pass over Hopkins' face as his colour returned and he replied, "A sensible precaution, Mr. Holmes," he said, lighting the candle. "I shall remain here on guard. Good luck, gentleman."

We walked on slowly with Holmes in the lead as the passage was just a bit narrow for the two of us to traverse it side by side. Once we were beyond the Inspector's earshot, I spoke to my companion. "You obviously recognized Hopkins' symptoms, Holmes. It was kind of you to offer him a plausible excuse to avoid a claustrophobic attack."

"I remembered hearing of the French discoveries of such a condition when I was a student back in the '70s. As I know Hopkins is not normally a man given to fear, I quickly surmised he had the condition. I do wonder that it did not manifest itself as we were descending the narrow passage between the walls."

This was one of those rare occasions when my medical knowledge complemented Holmes' memory of facts and I replied, "Often it is the type of enclosed space that affects the patient. Passing within man-made walls where there was a lit avenue of retreat was obviously tolerable. An earthen tunnel, which could prove unstable, with only one light source was obviously too much for him. Also, there may have been an incident in his past where such conditions first triggered his fears."

Holmes merely hummed in reply and pointed ahead. The tunnel was coming to an end. This area was wider, possibly used to store weapons or foodstuffs and there was a framework of what may have been for a bed at some time in the past. There were more paraffin lanterns on a shelf, which my companion checked for dust and signs of recent use. A ladder in good repair rose about ten feet to some sort of trap door. Holmes went first and threw open the door easily and silently, with nary a squeak to its hinges. I followed and we had emerged in a thick grove of oak trees and ground covered in sparse bracken along the eastern edge of St. Chad's Park.

Holmes examined the ground around the trap door, which, itself, was covered with bracken. While there were signs of disturbance, there were no readable footprints or any other trace of evidence.

I looked back toward the library and saw that we had gone perhaps fifty yards to the west. Holmes requested that I go back for Hopkins while he explored the ground between our exit and the building. We would meet up back at the pantry on the ground floor. I took the lantern and made my way back through the tunnel, shouting out a 'Hello' as soon as I saw the flicker of the Inspector's candle in the distance, knowing that he must be getting anxious by now. Relieved to see me, I further distracted his anxiety by explaining to him where we had come out and what Holmes' plan was. I gave him the lantern and he led the way back up to the landing that opened into the pantry. The pantry itself was a large storage area at the back of a kitchen that had seen little use in recent times, judging by the layer of dust on the counters. We brushed off a couple of chairs at a small table and awaited the detective's arrival.

We struck up a conversation, as we knew Holmes' thorough methods of search might take a while. Hopkins volunteered that he'd had a traumatic experience as a child while exploring a cave with cousins near his grandparents' farm. They were almost out of sight of the entrance, proceeding by candlelight, when one of his cousins thought he heard something up ahead. He threw a rock that bounced off the walls and set up a roar as hundreds of batwings began flapping and screaming past them. The boy holding the candle dropped it and it went out. The cloud of bats briefly blocked the daylight from the entrance and for several seconds young Stanley was plunged into total blackness with only screeches of both bats and boys to accompany him.

I sympathized with his plight. Such a traumatic experience could easily affect someone for life, I reassured him. I explained the intricacies of claustrophobia to him and it seemed to make him feel better, knowing that it was a medical condition and not an expression of cowardice.

Holmes arrived at that point and took up the now extinguished lantern, advising us not to mention it as we returned to O'Hare's office. The librarian was just finishing with a student as we entered and waved us to some seats off to one side. Holmes set the lantern on a small table and crossed his legs nonchalantly. When he was free, O'Hare walked out from behind his counter and asked if we'd found anything.

"Indeed, we have, sir," declared Holmes, almost jovially. "We've discovered a secret passage that leads down through the wall from the top floor clear to an underground tunnel, which would take someone wishing to get away out to the edge of St. Chad's Park."

"Extraordinary," exclaimed the gentleman. "Are you convinced then, that Bass and Douglas were murdered, and the killer got out that way?"

Holmes raised a forefinger, as if in caution, and replied, "Not as yet *convinced* as you say, but it confirms the possibility that someone other than a keyholder to the library could have been involved."

O'Hare seemed taken aback, "You thought someone with a key killed them?"

"It was a highly probable explanation," said Holmes. "Considering that once you lock the door for the night, no one can get in or out without a key. Douglas had one, but it's still with his effects. Who else has a key?"

O'Hare tilted his head in thought, then answered, "The Principal, of course, all of the heads, the groundskeeper and the warden. I believe that is all."

I had written these facts down at Holmes' instruction and then he said, "We shall have to determine if anyone of them had motives against both these individuals, which I admit, does not seem likely on the surface. The odds favour some connection with their participation in the Rugby league. Do students from other institutions come to use this library?"

O'Hare seemed to beam with pride, "Why, yes, Mr. Holmes. All the local students from Stratford to Brentwood have been known to come here for various types of research."

"So, it would not be uncommon for students from Ashlyn College over in Chigwell to be here?"

"I have noticed a few of their blue blazers from time to time, yes."

"Anyone on the day Douglas was killed?"

O'Hare thought for a moment, "I believe there were two Ashlyn students here together that afternoon."

Holmes brightened a bit at that, "Do you recall what time they left, or if they left at all?"

The Librarian shook his head, "If they didn't check anything out, Mr. Holmes, they could have walked right out the front door without my seeing them."

"Well," said Holmes as he stood, "it appears we have our work cut out for us. Good day, Mr. O'Hare. I've no doubt we'll speak again."

I noticed, as we followed Holmes out, that he left the lantern behind. However, we had not got halfway to the exit, when O'Hare appeared in his doorway, holding the object in his hand and, due to the atmosphere of the facility, emitting a stage whisper to inform us that we had forgotten it.

Holmes retreated a few steps, so as not to have to raise his voice and replied, "Oh, that is yours, or rather, the library's. You do not recognize it?"

O'Hare looked at it curiously and replied, "We have gas lighting throughout the building. There's no need for this. Where did you find it?"

"It was in the pantry of the old kitchen," said Holmes, pointing in that direction.

"Really?" the man commented. "Well, I suppose I'll just put it back there for now. Thank you, Mr. Holmes."

He turned in that direction and we continued our exit. Once outside I asked my companion, "What was that all about with the light?"

"Just trying to see how truthful our Librarian was. If he had been able to return the lantern without our help, it would be almost certain that he knew about the passage and its exit into the pantry where the lantern was kept."

Hopkins interjected, "Come, Mr. Holmes, you surely can't suspect that man capable of dispatching a youthful athlete like Bass, or a man of Douglas stature."

"As Watson will tell you, Inspector, I always attempt to eliminate the impossible until I am left with the most likely solution, no matter how improbable. It seemed a convenient time to test Mr. O'Hare and now we can move on to more probable avenues."

Chapter Four

Hopkins suggested that our next stop should be the Principal's office. He had already spoken with the man that morning, having called him in when the death was reported. Now he deemed a conversation with Holmes might prove more revealing.

My friend was in agreement. We were soon granted access to the office of Randolph Stockton-York, a wizened old man of seventy years, short, stocky, bald with a half circle of white fringe about his head and mutton chop whiskers to match. An older fashioned black suit featuring a tailcoat and dark green brocaded waistcoat, undoubtedly a bow to the college colours, completed the picture.

Behind him, as he sat in a high-backed ornately tapestried chair, hung a picture of Richard III, last king of the House of York. A nod, no doubt to his ancestry. There were four guest chairs facing his expansive desk. I sat between Holmes and Hopkins, which left my flatmate almost directly across from our host. I discreetly took out my notepad and prepared to record anything significant.

"Gentleman," began the man, in a grandfatherly tone, "I do hope you are not going to go about spreading rumours of *college killers* or a *haunted library*. Surely these were unfortunate, if coincidental, accidents that can be put to rest."

Holmes took control of the conversation, "I do not indulge in rumours, Principal, only in facts. At this point, the facts indicate that you have had two people murdered in your library. I will not bandy this information about until I have absolute proof, mind you. Once that proof is in hand, justice must be served. Surely you would not wish to taint the college's reputation by rumours of conspiracies or coverups? Who would trust an institution that puts the safety of its student body below a false reputation?"

The old man sat back, hands grasping the edge of his desk as he took this in. He twice started to speak and thought better of it, as the implication of Holmes' words swirled about in his mind. Finally, he conceded. Raising his right hand in conciliation, he spoke, "Ah, very well then, Mr. Holmes. As the Bard said, 'Truth will out'. I suppose it's better that we are seen as champions of justice than have our name sullied in the mud as deceivers of the public trust. King Richard would not approve." He pointed back over his shoulder at the painting and winked. Then he asked, "What can I do to help?"

Hopkins answered in his official capacity, "All we ask is permission to speak with any staff or student whom we may deem of interest in this matter. We also need to access college records."

"What records?" asked the Principal, cautiously.

Holmes answered. "Student records that may indicate disciplinary actions or low grades. Employment records of staff. Anything that could shine a light on who, if anyone, may have been involved. I should also explain that we will be looking at external sources as well. Rival institutions and the like."

Stockton-York raised his eyebrows at that suggestion and almost smiled as he considered it, "Yes, yes, that would certainly be a more likely explanation. Very well, gentlemen. I shall put the word out to the staff who will also inform their students that you are exploring the deaths in the library to ensure everyone's safety. Will that be satisfactory?"

Hopkins replied, "That is all we ask, Principal. Thank you. If you could call in your secretary to take us to your records room?"

The old academic rang a bell on his desk and a young woman appeared in the doorway at his summons. "Miss Tomkins, please show these gentlemen to the records room, and assist them with whatever they need. God save the King!"

The woman who responded was attractive with short brown hair that curled up just above her shoulders. She was also quite tall, perhaps five foot nine. She wore eyeglasses, but did not seem in the least self-conscious about them, as so many young women are. I presumed that, this being a Saturday, the Principal had called her in to assist when he learned of Douglas' death and the police investigation.

As we walked down the hall, I posed a medical concern I had to the young lady, "If I may, Miss, is the Principal quite all right? He seems a bit lost in time?"

She looked about and, once sure we could not be overheard, replied, "He has good days and bad ones, Doctor. He takes great pride in his York family roots and used to teach history before he went into administration full-time. They say his lectures on the Hundred Years War were quite emphatic. Lately he's been slipping away into the past more and more. It's not for me to say, but I believe he may be forced into retirement at the end of the term."

I nodded in sympathy and noted that Holmes also took an interest in this little tidbit. Arriving at the records room she unlocked it with a key on a ring hooked to the belt of her skirt containing several keys. Inside we found the walls were lined with wooden filing cabinets, each labelled and dating back to the very beginnings of the institution, over a century before. There was a table in the middle with six chairs around it. I noted that the older records took up far less drawer space than those of the last few decades. Hopkins immediately opened the current year's student file. I sought and found the relevant records. Holmes, however, chose to question the young woman who had escorted us.

"If I may, Miss Tomkins, did you know the student who died recently, Aloysius Bass?"

She crossed her arms over her chest and almost sneered, "Not as well as he would have liked, Mr. Holmes. I've never been one to fraternize with younger men, let alone musclebound, dim witted egotists like Bass."

"It sounds like he may have desired to change that," commented Holmes.

"I believe he may have seen me as a mere challenge, thinking he would be irresistible to someone like me. I represented a conquest he could not make."

"But he tried?" enquired the detective.

"Only once," she responded. "He attempted to corner me in my office one day after the Principal had left. When he reached for me, I grabbed his wrist, twisted his arm behind his back and kicked his feet out from under him. He hit his head on the desk and was too dizzy to stand straight away. That was when my fiancé, Alan, that is, Doctor Muncy, came by to pick me up. Alan took the situation in hand, lifted Bass up by the front of his shirt, threatened to expel him if he ever heard of him approaching me, or any other girl here, in such a manner again, then threw him out the door where he fell on his backside in the hallway in front of a handful of students who were just leaving. His embarrassment was complete and he ran out of the building."

"And he never bothered you again?"

"I never saw him again, Mr. Holmes. He obviously took my fiancé's threat to heart and kept his distance. That was a year ago now."

I spoke up and asked, "How did you manage to overpower him, Miss Tomkins? I understand he was quite an athlete."

She smiled and replied, "I grew up with three older brothers, Doctor, holding my own against them in our youth and learning from them as we aged."

Holmes thanked her and advised her that we would be a while and would let her know when we finished, so she could lock up again. Holmes had me pull Muncy's file while he retrieved that of Clifton Douglas. In the meantime, Hopkins was looking over Bass' file and also those of other students. I queried his research.

"These are the students whose names show up in Bass' file as having had run ins with him. There are three men and four women who've made complaints against him, including Miss Tomkins. There also a written reprimand from Doctor Muncy."

Holmes remarked, "With such a volatile personality and so many public complaints, one wonders how many victims remained silent out of fear? Our suspect pool grows significantly. We shall have to do something about that. Make sure you note all the contact information about these complainants, Inspector."

We spent the better part of an hour referencing and cross-checking anyone who may have held a grudge against Bass or Douglas, looking for someone each victim had in common. In several cases, Douglas came to Bass' defence, either as a witness or to supply an alibi. There was also a report of an altercation between Douglas and Muncy, shortly after the incident which Miss Tomkins had related to us.

Hopkins suddenly had another thought and left us to question Miss Tomkins again. When he returned, he sought out the files of two other students to add to those he had already taken.

"What have you found, Inspector?" queried Holmes.

"These are the students known for their practical jokes, according to Miss Tomkins," answered the Inspector. "There have been recent 'ghost sightings' and since we are not entertaining that possibility, there must be some human element involved. Practical jokers would be the most likely to perpetuate the ghost story and it may well be that somehow their paths crossed our victims."

"You're not suggesting that they would kill to keep their secret if they were caught in the act?" I asked.

"Just on the chance that the deaths are unrelated to each other," responded Hopkins. "It may be that Bass threatened to expose them. He may have confronted them with blackmail, a fight ensued and got out of hand. In the other case, if it was Douglas who caught them, he may have charged them with expulsion and they over-reacted, accidentally causing his fall against the table."

"That would not explain their twisted necks," observed Holmes.

Hopkins turned to me, "Doctor, would it be possible for Douglas to have fallen in such a way that his weight overcame the inertia of his head hitting the table edge and caused his neck to twist from the momentum?"

I thought back to the scene of the latest death and considered, then replied, "A mere fall from a standing position would not be sufficient, Inspector."

"What if he were pushed or thrown against the table?"

"It's not a likely outcome, but not impossible," I speculated.

Holmes spoke up, "So, you've added three more suspects to our tally, Inspector."

Hopkins shrugged his shoulders, "At the very least, we can talk to them and see what they may know about our victims. Men of that kind are usually well-informed."

"Oh, I quite agree," nodded Holmes. "As for myself, I believe a talk with Doctor Muncy is in order, as well as with Douglas' widow. Watson, I shall require your expertise on women for that interview."

I harrumphed, "You give me too much credit, Holmes, and not enough to yourself. You are quite capable of interviewing women successfully when you put your mind to it."

"Nevertheless ..." he implored.

"I shall be happy to accompany you, as always. What about the possibility of rival rugby players from Ashlyn?"

"I would prefer to play close to home for now, Doctor. The passion required for these murders seems far beyond that of winning a mere sporting cup."

Working with Miss Tomkins, we scheduled to meet with the students in question on Monday when they returned to college. She also consented to having us join her and Doctor Muncy later that afternoon, before dinner intervened. Holmes desired to question the widow of Douglas that evening as well, but Hopkins and I both prevailed upon him out of common courtesy, to give lady time to grieve and put off his questions until the following day.

Our interview with Doctor Muncy took place in the reception of the ladies' lodge where Miss Tomkins resided. Muncy was a barrel-chested fellow in his late twenties, clean-shaven with light brown hair worn slightly long, as is the fashion with some academics.

As Holmes, Hopkins and I sat down with him and his fiancée, Muncy jumped right to the heart of the matter. "From what I'm hearing, gentlemen, it sounds like you don't accept the *accident* theory of Bass' death, which leads you to suspect Douglas' death as well. I admit, had the order of their demise been reversed, I would have been less surprised. Bass had a temper and an ego. I could more readily accept his killing of a lecturer who threatened his place here."

I was taken aback by this frankness and replied, "Do you know of any threats he made?"

"I am not personally aware of any direct threats, though he made no secret of his displeasure at certain teachers, present company included."

Holmes spoke up and enquired, "After your altercation, did he ever confront you again?"

Muncy grinned, "He knew better, Mr. Holmes. I know it may not be my place to say it, but every once in a while a student comes along who needs to have his ears boxed. He was well aware that I was not afraid of him and gave me a wide berth."

Holmes nodded in appreciation at his honesty and continued, "Were there any other staff members who felt as you do?"

The Doctor shook his head, "Not to the extent that they would kill him. Douglas did his best to keep him under control because of his skill on the rugby field, but if you ask me, that talent was overrated. He was not really a team player. That will only take you so far. Against the better colleges he was more a hindrance than a help."

"Could Douglas have confronted him and the argument have escalated into a killing in self-defence?" asked Holmes.

"Douglas would certainly have had the advantage in a fair fight," replied Muncy. "Though I doubt Bass would ever fight fair. I suppose, if it came to that, Douglas could have done it. I could only imagine it would have been an extreme circumstance, like putting down a wild animal. Even then, I would expect him to come forward and explain himself and not stage an accident."

"One never knows how a person will react when confronted with a traumatic situation," said the detective. "The most rational and intelligent man may succumb to any number of emotions and perform incredibly out of character, when controlled by fear and panic.

"Tell me, do you have any thoughts on who might wish Douglas dead?"

Miss Tomkins spoke up at that, "Clifton was well-liked by his students. Perhaps too much so by some of the women. There were some rumours, but nothing substantiated. The only complaints I've heard about him have been from parents of athletes who thought their sons weren't getting enough field time."

"Interesting," commented Holmes. "Was he the flirtatious sort, in spite of his marriage?"

"Not exactly, Mr. Holmes. I never saw any overt action on his part. I never witnessed any discouragement either. I think he welcomed the attention. However, I don't believe he ever acted upon it. Not to my knowledge anyway."

Muncy chimed in, "He's certainly never been caught at any inappropriate behaviour. He would have been dismissed immediately. The Principal and Board of Trustees would never have stood for it."

We then changed the course of the discussion toward any students who might have had grudges against either Bass or Douglas. The most notable revelation was that all of the practical jokers we had discovered, had been involved in fights with Bass.

We took our leave of the young couple and decided to arrange lodgings for the night at the same hotel where Hopkins was staying for the duration of the investigation. First however, Holmes expressed a need to return to Baker Street, so the two of us caught the next train back to Liverpool Street. We packed a few clothes and informed Mrs. Hudson that we would be gone for two or three days. I packed my medical bag and my old Webley revolver, just in case. Holmes had a second carpet bag to complement his overnight suitcase. As we walked out, our kind landlady handed me some sandwiches wrapped in paper, knowing Holmes' penchant for forgetting to eat. Something I took advantage of, on the return train. We were back at the Bentley Hotel by eight thirty and agreed to a plan Holmes had outlined for us for the evening.

Chapter Five

Chadwell Heath did not have an overabundance of pubs or other drinking establishments. Consequently, Holmes suggested Hopkins and I go off together, while he, in one of his disguises from his carpet bag, went about in the other direction. Our goal was to discreetly infiltrate the gossip mongers and see what the locals thought about the death at the college and their theories on what may have happened.

It was after eleven o'clock at night when we returned to our hotel. Hopkins and I had heard numerous opinions. Many believed it was accidental as reported, while others were convinced it was the ghost of Sir Osbert. Some thought it was an argument with one of his players that escalated into violence and an unintentional death. One old wag, for the price of a drink, offered the opinion that it was one of Douglas' jilted female students and added his opinion that women should not be allowed to attend the same school as men.

After we shared these with Holmes, he added some additional viewpoints he had gleaned. These included: friends of Bass exacting revenge on the coach for killing Bass; Douglas' wife did it, after finding out about her husband's affair with a student; the boyfriend, brother or father of some female Douglas had wronged, killed him in revenge.

The interesting thing about all of the theories we had heard was that, except for the one about Douglas killing Bass, everyone seemed to accept Bass' death as accidental. The local populous seemed to agree with the official report that he fell off the ladder, in spite of his reputation. The general feeling was that someone out to kill Bass would use a more reliable method.

At this Holmes invoked one of his adages, "There is nothing more deceptive than an obvious fact.[1] We've gleaned many points to ponder, gentlemen. Tomorrow we shall ..."

A sharp knock on the door interrupted his conclusion and Hopkins answered it. It was Doctor Muncy.

"Gentlemen, I think you should come with me. There is something I'm sure you'll want to investigate."

"What is it?" asked Holmes.

"The ghost of Sir Osbert is wandering the library. Alice and I saw him through the windows as I walked her home."

*****

We all looked at each other sceptically. Hopkins was the first to move. As a sworn officer of the law, he was duty bound to investigate any possibility of foul play. I followed out of curiosity and Holmes looked forward to debunking this superstition once and for all.

We arrived at the library in mere minutes. As we approached, we could see a candlelit figure on the second floor, passing back and forth across the windows in medieval dress and wearing the blue mantle of a member of the Order of the Garter. We also noted that the librarian was just about to enter the front door. Holmes had Muncy wait outside and keep observing the actions of the figure in the window while Hopkins ran to join O'Hare in hopes of apprehending whoever or whatever that apparition on the top floor turned out to be.

In the meantime, Holmes motioned to me to follow him to where we knew the tunnel exit was located. We lay in wait

---

[1] Quote appears in the 1891 adventure *The Boscombe Valley Mystery* submitted by Arthur Conan Doyle.

upon the hinge side where we would not be visible until our prey was up and out of the hole. Fortunately, a three-quarter moon provided enough light through the trees that, being this close, allowed us to see. My companion had me draw my revolver, just to dissuade any objections to our trap.

It was just as well I did so. When the first man out of the tunnel realized we were there, he started to yell for his companion to go back. My order to 'halt or be shot', dissuaded the second fellow from retreating and they both raised their hands in submission. Holmes looked down the tunnel. Seeing no light, he determined that these were the only two and ordered them back to the library, through the front door this time.

The two culprits were young, likely students in their late teen-aged years. Both were of average build and clean shaven. One, a redhead with freckled face and hazel eyes, was doing well at hiding his anxiety. He exuded a confidence that seemed determined he could talk his way out of trouble. The other fellow, with short black hair, and fearful brown eyes, was shaking with nerves. Holmes sat them down in O'Hare's office and sent me up to get the rest of our party.

When we came back down, Doctor Muncy immediately confronted the boys by name, "Colm, Walter, what have you two been up to? Was Frederick with you?"

Colm, the redhead and obvious leader of this little pack, replied, "Just the two of us Doctor. Freddy didn't have the stomach for it tonight."

"The stomach for what?" ordered Hopkins, after introducing himself as an Inspector from Scotland Yard. Walter, the timid fellow, buried his head in his hands at this revelation, then looked up and blurted out at his companion, "I told you it was too soon! Freddy was right! We should have waited until the heat died down."

"We didn't mean no harm, sir," he said, answering Hopkins. "It was just a joke."

"You broke into my library to play a joke! The night after a murder?" cried out O'Hare, incensed at the gall of the two youngsters.

"Murder!" cried Walter. "Oh my God! Colm, what did you drag me into?"

Colm, not quite so cocky now, tried to be defiant, but his voice betrayed his fear at this revelation. "We didn't know anything about a murder! We thought that Douglas had a heart attack or tripped and hit his head. We just wanted to give the superstitious folk more gossip by moving around old Osbert's mannequin. You know, pretending the ghost was still out and about and maybe responsible."

Holmes, who had been oddly quiet, had been observing the scene and finally spoke up, "Just where were you two last night, around ten when the library closed."

Walter rushed to speak, "I was home, sir! You can ask my parents. I didn't have anything to do with what happened to Mr. Douglas."

The detective turned his steel grey eyes on Colm and the boy answered, a little more confidently now, "I was over at Freddy's house 'til near eleven. His parents can vouch for that. His father talked me into joining a family card game."

"And after that?"

"Straight home, sir. I live right next door to Freddy. It's over on Southern Way near St. Edward's Church, about a mile east of here."

Holmes ascertained that the boys had been pulling this prank for two years now, ever since they started attending the college. Then he asked, "How did you find the secret panel and the tunnel?"

Walter started to answer, but Colm jumped in and confessed, "I did it. I snuck into the kitchen one day to see if I could find something to eat and went into the pantry. I went to light the lantern and when I lit my match it flickered like there was some bit of wind. I checked around and found the passage."

The look on Walter's face indicated that this was not at all the truth, but a glare from his companion dissuaded him from contradicting the story. Holmes let it pass and finally asked, "Does anyone else know about it, besides you two and your friend Frederick? Have you seen signs of anyone else using it?"

"Just the three of us is all," replied the redhead. "We swore each other to secrecy. I've never seen anything that looked like anyone else had been in there for a long time."

"Is that right, Walter?" asked the detective. "How about you? Have you seen signs of anyone else using it?"

The lad cocked his head to one side and said, "No, sir. I wasn't looking for any such signs, so there may have been. But, if so, it weren't obvious."

"*Wasn't*, obvious," corrected O'Hare. The librarian side of him automatically reacting to improper grammar.

Holmes asked a few more questions, then turned the boys over to Hopkins who enlisted Doctor Muncy's help to take the boys to their respective homes and verify their alibis. My companion and I stayed with O'Hare to discuss the matter.

O'Hare broke into a coughing fit and we retreated to the pantry for some water. Sitting at the table there, Holmes waited for the man to settle and then asked, "Does Colm, or any of the others, have older brothers who attended here?"

"Why yes, Colm's older brother, Devon, graduated from here about four years ago. Why?"

"Were there any incidents or ghost sightings during the time he was in attendance?" asked the detective.

O'Hare raised his eyes to the ceiling in thought as he searched his memory, then lowered his head to face us, "Actually there was, as I recall. During Devon's graduation year there were a handful of incidents. A few times there were books piled on the tables with Sir Osbert's mantle thrown over them. At least twice it was reported that someone had seen a ghostly figure in the second floor windows late at night. One time all the old Latin bibles were laid out upon a table, every one turned to the 23rd Psalm and Osbert's shield had been taken off the wall and laid atop them, as if protecting them from something."

Holmes nodded, "Any activity of that sort recently?"

O'Hare shook his head, "Just the movement of the mannequin on some nights like tonight. Though I did find Sir Osbert's broadsword on the floor one time. Next to his shield on the third floor. Between the shield and the wall. Usually it's on the first floor, with his armour."

Holmes pondered that a moment, "Just out of curiosity, which direction was the sword pointing?"

"It was perpendicular to the shield, aimed at the wall with the point right up against the panelling."

"Odd, but not impossible. When was this?"

"It was there on the Monday morning after the Saturday we found Bass' body."

Holmes made a note of that, then declared as he rose to leave, "I believe we've gleaned enough for one evening, Watson. Just one more thing, Mr. O'Hare. Where did Mr. Douglas go to church?"

Chapter Six

The next morning, Holmes insisted that I join him for Sunday services at St. Chad's Church. We arrived early and found many parishioners outside, discussing one of two subjects; the death of Clifton Douglas, or the celebration preparations for the dedication of St. Chad's as a parish church. Apparently the following month there was to be an official recognition as a parish in its own right and no longer the daughter church of Dagenborn Parish of the Church of England.

Naturally our interests lay in the discussions and theories regarding the latest victim in the library. To obtain as much information as possible, we split up and attempted to overhear as many conversations as feasible. In an effort not to be inundated with questions, Holmes had continued his disguise from the previous night and told anyone who spoke to him that he was just a businessman passing through.

In this manner, he was able to circulate rather freely. I, on the other hand, concentrated my efforts around those folks who were comforting the widow Douglas who, in spite of her mourning attire and veil, seemed quite attractive and younger than her husband. I heard many condolences, but also whispered remarks behind her back that seemed to reinforce what we had gleaned about her husband's reputation. Some even went so far as to speculate that it was a male relative or friend of a spurned student who had 'done him in'.

When the bell tolled for folks to enter, Holmes and I drifted back toward each other and happened upon Orson O'Hare. He greeted me warmly but did not recognize my companion until Holmes spoke and requested that he not use his name. The librarian nodded and merely said, "I did not recognize you, sir. Welcome to St. Chad's." As they shook hands, I saw Holmes inspecting the man in that surreptitious manner of his and I followed suit, though I am not nearly so observant as my friend. The only difference I saw in O'Hare was him being in his Sunday best clothes, wearing a fine gold watch with some sort of medallion on the fob and an ornate ring on his finger. We entered together and Holmes, in spite of the circumstances, was in fine voice for the hymns. Afterward we bid O'Hare 'farewell' and headed to a nearby pub where we had agreed to meet Hopkins for lunch.

The Inspector had not accompanied us to church that morning, having to report to the Yard. Now he was back and anxious to hear if we had learned anything. I repeated what I had shared with Holmes about rumours of infidelity and revenge and then my companion spoke.

"As a general consensus, Douglas was treated with respect for his office and his record as the rugby coach. However, the man himself seemed to have fallen short of being held in esteem. Many appear to feel sorry for Mrs. Douglas more for putting up with his philandering all these years than for losing her husband. Some exhibited happiness that she is now free to pursue a more worthy spouse, for she is well-liked among the parishioners."

"What does that do for your theory of the crime, Mr. Holmes?" asked Hopkins.

"Certainly, it presents a possible motive," answered the detective. "Though not one that connects this killing with Bass and I am loathe to separate the two as yet. I should like to call upon the widow this afternoon and would prefer to do so in an official capacity, rather than appear as some interloper upon her mourning. Would you be amenable to come with us at three o'clock, Inspector?"

It was agreed upon and at three o'clock we were at a neat Tudor home in Portland Gardens, just north of St. Chad's Park. We were greeted at the door by a strapping fellow of nearly six feet in height. We recognized him as the man who had escorted the widow Douglas to church that morning. From what we had overheard, we knew this to be her brother.

"Yes, gentlemen? May I help you?" he asked, in a tone that clearly conveyed he would brook no superfluous intrusion upon his sister's mourning. This, being an official visit, caused Hopkins to speak for us as he held up his identification.

"Good day, sir. I am Inspector Hopkins of Scotland Yard. This is Sherlock Holmes and Dr. Watson. We would like to ask Mrs. Douglas a few questions so we might complete the official report on her husband's death."

"Can't this wait, Inspector? My sister has had a very trying day."

Before Hopkins could answer, Holmes spoke up, "Perhaps you could answer the majority of our questions, sir? Then the intrusion upon your sister would be minimal."

The brother looked back over his shoulder, then acquiesced, "Very well. We can talk in the dining room. He let us in, showed us the way, then left us momentarily to inform his sister what he was doing so she could rest. When he returned, he sat at the head of the table with Holmes and me on one side and Hopkins on the other. "My wife is seeing to Helen's needs for now, but I'd like to hurry this along. The undertaker is coming by at four to go over funeral arrangements."

The Inspector had his notebook out, as did I, and he asked, "First of all, what is your name, sir?"

"Sherman, Calvin Sherman."

"And where do you live?"

"Enfield. I'm a design engineer for the Royal Small Arms Factory there in Lea Valley."

"When did you arrive here?"

"I received a telegram from Helen around noon yesterday. My wife and I arrived on the four o'clock train. Why all these questions about me? What do you really want to know?"

"Just being thorough, Mr. Sherman. We need to account for everyone's whereabouts at the time of the death."

"You're making this sound like a murder investigation. Are you saying Cliff didn't die by accident?"

Holmes answered that in a soft voice, "The police surgeon's report leaves some room for interpretation. Are you aware of any enemies with whom your brother-in-law may have associated?"

Sherman leaned back in his chair, his hands on the edge of the table, then looked up at the ceiling momentarily. Finally, he bent forward, hands clasped in front of him as his chin hovered above them. Keeping his voice low he replied, "If you've been investigating a possible crime, then I'm sure you have heard rumours of infidelity. I confronted Cliff on this very matter some months ago. He assured me that, while there have been some female students exhibiting infatuations toward him over the years, he had never responded and was absolutely faithful to Helen. I believed he was sincere. I also made it plain to him that, should it prove otherwise, he would answer to me."

"Was there a reason for your scepticism?" asked the detective.

He looked toward the door and then back to us before he replied, "Helen was one of those students fifteen years ago."

In my mind that solved the reason for her youthful appearance. She must have been at least ten years younger than Douglas.

Hopkins, without judgement, took up the official inquiry and asked, "For the record, Mr. Sherman, where were you on Friday night?"

Our host stared at the Inspector, "I understand you must ask the question, sir. However, I assure you, I would not make my sister a widow. Cliff may have found himself requiring substantial medical attention after the thrashing I would have given him. But he would still be alive. As to my whereabouts, my wife and I were visiting neighbours for dinner and an evening of whist."

Hopkins made a note of the details, then asked one more question, "Are you aware of any dealings that Douglas may have had with the student who died in the library two months ago, Aloysius Bass?"

"I don't know if I ever heard the name. I just heard that one of the rugby players had died of a fall from a book ladder. Do you think there's a connection?"

"Just an odd coincidence, and I detest coincidence," replied the Inspector, who looked at Holmes. My friend merely nodded and then said, "I believe that's all we require from you. Mr. Sherman. If we could just ask your sister one or two questions, we'll conclude."

"I would ask that you not bring up any issues of infidelity, Inspector. This is hardly the time to make her face that cruel inference."

Holmes spoke up, "If I may, Inspector? Mr. Sherman, I merely have two things to ask your sister and I assure you that neither will infer any misbehaviour on her husband's part."

Sherman agreed and when we were led to the parlour where the widow and her sister-in-law were quietly drinking tea, Holmes took the lead, after introductions.

"Mrs. Douglas, I assure you that we do not wish to intrude upon your troubles. We have two questions that will assist the doctor in his final report, to enable your husband to be released for burial."

She sat up a little straighter and dabbed her tear-streaked cheek. With a sniffle she bravely replied, 'Yes, Mr. Holmes, what is it? "

"First, has your husband seemed unduly worried about anything lately, any nervousness, or has he seemed distracted?"

"No, sir. Just the opposite. He has been quite cheerful. His team is doing well and he was looking forward to the summer holidays and a trip we were planning to the Continent."

"Very good, madam. Just one other point. Has his health been quite regular? No dizzy spells or incidents showing a lack of coordination, dropping things, tripping or losing his balance?"

"He was in the peak of health, Mr. Holmes. He was quite vigorous and of good stamina."

Here her voice broke, and she could not help but let out a sob. I spoke up, knowing that Holmes had his answers. "Thank you, Mrs. Douglas, we just needed to rule out the possibility of any medical symptoms of his brain or heart. I am confident now that tripping on the rug would have been accidental and not due to any medical condition. With your permission, we shall take our leave. You have our deepest condolences, madam."

In her state, she merely waved us away and we left. Holmes suggested another trip to the library to re-examine the scene of each crime. Hopkins said we could pick up Douglas' keys from the police surgeon, but Holmes waved aside the suggestion. "No need to bother the man on a Sunday afternoon. I suggest we enter by way of the secret tunnel." Noting the look on the Inspector's face, he amended his statement, "That is, I shall enter through the tunnel and let you and Watson in by the front door."

When Holmes let the Inspector and I in, the first thing I noticed was that the suit of armour had been moved to the opposite side of the entrance hall. I queried Holmes who speculated that it had likely been moved by the boys as part of their prank to continue the legend of the ghost of Sir Osbert. Then I pointed out that the sword was missing. "Remember, O'Hare told us the sword had been moved before. Up to the top floor next to the shield."

"It's not upstairs," said Holmes.

"How can you know that?" asked Hopkins

Holmes pointed across the room, "Look there!"

We followed his gesture and there, in front of the door to the Librarian's office, was Sir Osbert's broadsword, driven into the floor like a stake. We walked over and Holmes knelt to examine it. The blade was facing the doorway and the handle was angled slightly toward the front door. The blade itself was clean and polished bright. Holmes judged that it was sunk about two inches into the floorboards. It had struck about a foot in front of O'Hare's door, directly in the centre between the jambs.

"It would require someone of considerable strength to drive the sword in that deep," noted Hopkins.

"Not necessarily," responded Holmes. "The angle actually points to the method. This was not held in two hands and thrust straight downward, as one might expect. The fact that it is on an angle indicates the wielder circled it around in a throwing motion and built up momentum so that its own weight would add to the centrifugal force and allow for deeper penetration. The culprit could have added even more momentum by getting a running start."

"But why? And why here, at the librarian's door?" asked the Inspector.

Holmes responded as he yanked the broadsword from the oak floor, which took considerable effort, I might add. "My primary concern is 'who', at the moment. Certainly knowing 'why' could help us narrow that down, but, speculating upon motive for such an unusual act would be too time-consuming without further data. Let us consider what we do know. Besides the three of us, and now O'Hare and Muncy, we know that Colm, Walter and Frederick know about the passage."

I spoke up and offered, "I'm sure Colm and Walter are being kept under strict observation by their parents after last night. So that leaves Frederick."

Holmes tilted his head, "That we know of. I'm convinced that Colm was lying about discovering the passage himself. I think it much more plausible the secret has been passed down from form to form and that Colm's brother, Devon, likely told him about it."

"That would certainly account for all the reported sightings over the years," said Hopkins.

"Yes, and the fact that the tunnel seems well-maintained. Unlike some passage that has lain unused for centuries. For now, however, Frederick is our primary suspect for this act. But that does not address the larger crime. Who is our killer, or killers?"

That piqued my interest, for I had only been thinking in the singular, "You think the boys may have ganged up on Bass and Douglas, Holmes?"

"A consideration we cannot discount at this time. I believe a visit to this Frederick fellow is in order."

*****

The three of us, after checking the notes we had taken from the student files, made our way to the home of Frederick Grayson. His parents bore out his alibi as having been home with them and his friend Colm on the night Douglas was killed. Still, Inspector Hopkins used his authority to insist that we be allowed to speak with the lad alone.

Freddy, as he was referred to by his friends and parents, was very tall. I would put him at six feet and four inches. He was very thin and seemingly non-athletic. I should say he was still growing into his height, like a young colt awkwardly finding its footing before developing into a thoroughbred.

We met with the lad in his room where he folded his spindly arms and legs into a chair while we stood above him. Hopkins opened the questioning.

"We have heard from your parents and witnesses that you were here last Friday evening and did not go to the library. Correct?"

The lad's Adam's apple bobbed as he nodded and put great effort into not wringing his hands. Which was only partially successful. Hopkins continued.

"But you have been in the library at times when it was not open to the public by way of the secret tunnel."

His eyes widened at the fact that we were aware of the tunnel, then he bowed his head and quietly said, "Yes, sir."

"Have you ever gone into the library through the tunnel on your own, or were you always in the company of Colm and Walter?"

"Oh, I'd never go in there by myself, sir. Not with the ghost of Sir Osbert walkin' about."

Holmes jumped in, "Come now, Master Frederick, surely you've never seen such an apparition?"

The boy cocked his head and thought before answering, "Well, no, I haven't actually seen him. But there have been plenty of times when he made his presence known. Moving things about and such. One time, when we went to leave, his shield was on the floor leaning up against the passage door, like it was trying to block our way."

Holmes pursed his lips and asked, "When you made these little jaunts into the library, did you always stay together, or did you separate from each other to perform different mischiefs?"

"Usually we stayed together, but sometimes we split up, though I always stayed with Wally while Colm went off by himself."

"How long have you been engaged in these little shenanigans?"

"Since we met up in our first year. Once we got to be friends, Colm showed me and Wally the tunnel and we would sneak in and just move things around or put books out of order. We never damaged anything."

The detective nodded and then stated, "... and it was Colm's brother Devon, who told him about the tunnel. Does anyone else know?"

The lad seemed a bit taken aback by that. "Colm told you that? He made us swear an oath that we would never reveal who told us and we would have to all agree who we would pass that knowledge on to after we graduated."

He seemed crestfallen, "Well, now that you know, I guess the game is up."

"Just one more question," said Holmes. "Do you have any opinion as to who might wish to kill Aloysius Bass or Dean Douglas?"

"Kill!?" exclaimed the young student. "I thought they both died in accidental falls. You don't think we had anything to do with that do you? Oh, my God! No!"

He started to stand as if he needed to be upright to defend himself, but Holmes placed his hands on the lad's shoulders and kept him seated.

"It's all right, my boy. Calm down. We are not accusing you. I just wish your opinion, if you have one."

After a few deep breaths, Frederick put his head in his hands as he thought. After several seconds he looked up at us and spoke. "I don't know about Douglas, but there were rumours about Bass and some girl. She left the school in the middle of the term last year and I think I heard that she died. Maybe someone was getting revenge?"

The three of us looked at each other at this revelation. Holmes nodded at Hopkins and the Inspector told the young fellow that we were finished for now, but he was not to discuss our conversation with anyone.

After we left the Grayson home, we decided to split up as we did the previous evening and see what gossip mongers had to say about this tidbit of information. When we rendezvoused back at the hotel, we gathered in Holmes' room to share our findings.

Conflicting testimony seemed to rule the evening, a few theories about the ghost and other parties who may have had a motive. One thing that we had heard in common was about the death the previous year of 'the Lancaster girl'. The first name varied from Abbey to Angel, to Virginia, all religious connotations, but no confirmation as to the fact. Some blamed Bass, others thought Douglas was involved. After we had discussed our findings, Holmes suggested we look into her school records in the morning after he 'smoked a pipe or two upon it tonight'.

However, the next morning brought an early message from O'Hare. He wished to see Holmes and I, in the Library immediately, without Inspector Hopkins.

Chapter Seven

Holmes made no mention of this message to the Inspector, as Hopkins received a telegram that morning, requiring him to return to Scotland Yard immediately regarding another, more urgent case.

"Let me know if you find anything, Holmes," he stated as he bade us goodbye on his way to the railway station. Holmes and I then proceeded to the library, instead of the college records room as planned, to see what was so urgent in the gentleman's mind.

Entering the library, we were surprised to see that the sword had been returned to the position where we had found it the day before, impaled into the floor at O'Hare's office door. We walked around it and looked in upon the man.

O'Hare leaned back in the chair behind his desk and bid us enter. There was no panic on his face, as he simply took off his spectacles and nonchalantly cleaned them. He placed them back on his face and looked at my companion, "What took you so long, Mr. Holmes, and was it really necessary to impale a sword at my door?" Then he added, "Please, both of you, do sit down."

I was certainly confused at that statement. Holmes, however, immediately took a seat and I followed suit. Holmes replied to the librarian in a conversational tone.

"To answer your second question first, Mr. O'Hare, I did not plant the sword in the floor at your door. We and the

Inspector found it that way yesterday afternoon. I believe Colm's older brother, Devon, may be responsible, but I have not had the time to test that theory.

"Secondly, I do not make accusations until my deductions leave me no choice. While I did not eliminate you completely, I did not consider you a strong suspect at first, due to the age difference between you and the victims. You also passed my little test with the lantern from the pantry. However, you did slip and say 'murder' when we confronted the boys Saturday night. Even now, while I have no doubt as to your involvement in these killings, I have been only able to speculate on your motives. It is for this reason that I am glad that Inspector Hopkins was unable to join us. I should like you to speak freely, sir, without fear of the official police taking down what you say to use against you."

The gentleman gazed toward the ceiling and took a deep breath, followed by a vicious cough, which took some time to recover from before answering. "So, the sword wasn't your doing? I thought it a message meant to warn me you were on to me. That's why I sent for you, to tell my story before it was too late. I didn't think Devon was in town, but I suppose he may have come home for the weekend." He stopped and then gave a snort of laughter, which set off a long, drawn out coughing fit.

Finally, he was able to speak again, "Hah! Tis probably the ghost of old Osbert telling me he's coming for me. It matters little what you do, Mr. Holmes. My time on this mortal coil will likely be at an end long before a trial and sentence can be carried out."

"Tuberculosis?" I speculated sympathetically, as I observed him from a medical viewpoint.

His Irish heritage slipped through his speech as he answered, "Aye, Dr. Watson. Six months, maybe less they tell me, is all I have. T'was time for me to act, while I still had the strength for it."

Holmes had crossed his legs and steepled his fingers beneath his chin during this exchange. Now he folded his hands across his waistcoat and quietly spoke, "You have taken on the role of vigilante, meting out punishment where others have failed to act. But were their deaths fit for their crimes?"

"Death was too good for them!" said the librarian in a cold, measured voice that belied his normal demeanour. "But I did not have the power to sentence them to long living deaths in prison and Caldwell would never bring shame upon his *alma mater* by even investigating a student or faculty member."

"We've heard rumours about Bass, but why Douglas?" I queried, fearing the answer even as I asked, for O'Hare's wrath even now seemed to ooze from his pores like heat from a fever.

"You've discovered Bass' reputation among the women of our fair land, no doubt. While most have suffered his ultimate rejection in silence after being courted by him for a time, there was one lass, a poor innocent creature, whom he could not win over by his winning looks and smooth tongue. Angelina Lancaster was her name and a fitting one it was, for she had the looks and gracious heart of an Angel of God. Her father had died when she was quite young and she had no brothers. I was probably the closest thing she had to a male protector, for she spent hours each week here in the library. Not only was she learning on her own, but also reading to younger children and helping them. I've no doubt she would have become a fine teacher.

"But Bass would not take 'no' for an answer. One day, last spring, he cornered her alone after school, overpowered the poor creature and dragged her to a cloakroom to have his way with her. She was too delicate to have left any mark upon him of her struggles to get away and when she reported it, not only did Bass deny it, but Douglas swore that his star player was practicing with him on the other side of the college at the time. He was just as guilty as Bass. Caldwell completed the travesty when he refused to press charges and admonished her for her lies.

"Well, gentlemen, you can imagine how she felt. She could not return to school to face her attacker in the halls every day. There wasn't money enough from her mother's meagre income to go away to another school. Then, the cruellest blow of all hit her. She found herself to be with child."

"The poor girl!" I exclaimed.

He closed his eyes and bowed his head upon his hand propped up by the arm of his chair, his thumb and fingers pressed to his eyes. It was several seconds before he could speak. At last he looked up, eyes on the verge of tears.

"It was too much for her. The thought of bearing that monster's child was more than she could take. They found her body, three miles from here, drowned in Fairlop Waters. A suicide note was left in her bedroom, again accusing Bass and again it was ignored by the police."

"So, you took matters into your own hands," suggested Holmes.

"Something had to be done!" cried O'Hare, slamming his fist on the arm of his chair. Another coughing fit hit him and it was several seconds before he regained his composure and continued, "Had I still owned my old service revolver I would have shot the beast on sight! Instead, I concentrated on seeing to the needs of Angelina's mother, who was so distraught she eventually needed to be admitted to an asylum."

"Yes," commented Holmes. "I had discerned that you were a former military person by your bearing, and by the ring you wear on Sundays. Your watch fob indicates some time spent in the orient. I presume that is where you learned your hand to hand combat skills?"

"Correct, Mr. Holmes, I was stationed in Hong Kong for two years and was able to incorporate Chinese fighting skills into my training. It has always helped me to triumph over larger opponents. I was hoping the *accidents* I staged would cover up that fact, but you were too persistent. You and that Inspector Hopkins!"

"Why kill them in the library?" I asked. "Surely that was your greatest risk."

Holmes replied to that, "You should know the answer to that, Watson. How many times have you brought up the ghost of Sir Osbert? Even among sceptics like myself, the reputation of a location can effect perception. Accidents can happen due to an as yet to be explained condition, other than the ghosts who get blamed for it. Tricks of the light or uneven surfaces or the like. Tell me, Mr. O'Hare, at least some of the recent sightings of Sir Osbert's ghost were the result of your doing, were they not?"

The librarian allowed himself a faint smirk as he answered, "Not at first, Mr. Holmes. There have been unexplained phenomena over the centuries of course, but when Colm and his gang started the latest rash of events. I merely took up the mantle, so to speak, and perpetuated the myth."

"Appropriate," responded Holmes, "as the blue velvet mantle of the Order of the Garter is a key piece of the wardrobe on the mannequin of Sir Osbert's likeness. Its placement on a rolling stand must have made it quite easy to move it past the windows with strategically placed candlelight to fool observers outside the building. If anyone who had a key passed by, you could merely duck into the secret passage, emerge outside and appear to arrive with all the other curiosity seekers."

The old man shook his head, "Only once, sir. On all other occasions I merely went home and waited to be called upon, thus establishing my alibi. Finally, the time came when conditions were right to strike. I took note of Bass' struggles as he studied for upcoming examinations that would keep him off the rugby team if he failed. He was oblivious of my knowledge of Angelina and his crime and was eager to accept my offer of assistance to help him prepare for the exams. We agreed to meet one night at closing time, so that he could maintain his reputation as being non-studious. I had placed books he needed on the top shelf, requiring him to ascend the ladder. As I stood beneath, I could barely contain my anxiety as he came down, step by step, until he reached that fateful rung where my hands could wrench his feet away and make him fall. He cried out on his way down, but this library is deadly quiet, as you know. He hit his head on the floor, though still conscious when I fell upon him, driving my knee into his kidney to knock the wind from him. I wrapped my hands around his skull and whispered Angelina's name into his ear. It was the last thing he heard before the fatal twist was applied to his neck."

"I presume you used a similar pretence with Douglas," commented my companion. "I would wager that you also incorporated the use of Sir Osbert's blue mantle in your attack and that was how the threads came to be under his fingernails."

"Yes," answered the librarian. "I suggested the end of the day meeting and made sure everyone was gone and the doors locked. I told him I thought I knew the real killer of Bass and hinted it was one of his other players. I arranged to meet him on the third floor where I could expound my theory at the scene of the crime. He was sitting at the table when I arrived carrying the cloth, thinking it could give me an advantage over his greater size. He had turned to greet me when I tossed a book onto the table as I came up from behind his shoulder. When he turned back to look at the volume, I threw the mantle over his head and jumped on his back with all my weight, using my hands to force his head onto the table's edge and repeated my cry of Angelina's name as I finished him off.

"I spoke her name, so that they would have that flash of memory as their last before death. The final thought that would be ever present as they stood before heaven's Judgement Seat."

I chose not to question him regarding his own thoughts of his position on that looming day, for I was sure he saw himself as God's instrument of justice.

Holmes and I sat in silence. I felt as if I had just sat through a moving performance of the Scottish Play[1]. O'Hare, himself, seemed likewise, emotionally drained. My friend sat perfectly still, deep in thought as he closed his eyes.

At last he opened them, stared grimly at the elder man and spoke, "There are yet two more people on your list."

The librarian lowered his head in a slow nod, "Just one, Mr. Holmes. The Principal is a senile old fool who thinks the War of the Roses is still going on and that his Yorkist background automatically condemns all Lancastrians as the enemy. He needs to be removed from office, but his mind is too deteriorated to hold responsible. I do wish, however, that I

---

[1] Shakespeare's *MacBeth* is often referred to in this fashion, due to superstitions surrounding the play and a curse coming upon anyone who speaks its name aloud.

could have remained at liberty long enough to exact justice on that scoundrel of a coroner, Caldwell."

Holmes then stood and made an extraordinary statement, "If I may elicit your word of honour not to take any more vigilante actions, Mr. O'Hare, will you allow me to handle the matter?"

"Holmes!" I cried in protest as I also rose.

The detective turned to me, "Watson, dear fellow, do you not agree that this poor man is not a danger to society? That his only *crime* has been to render justice where none had been served?"

"But, *murder*, Holmes?" I questioned.

He placed his hand upon my shoulder, "Put yourself in his place, my friend. What if the victim had been your poor Mary?"

My right hand automatically stole to my left ring finger, where I could still feel the indentations left by my wedding band, now a cherished keepsake in my jewellery box. The pain of her illness and death of but two years before, still lingered strong in my memories. His suggestion wrenched at my heart and I could not deny my empathy for O'Hare's plight.

"What are you proposing, Holmes?" I sighed.

He clapped my shoulder and turned back toward the librarian, "We do not mention this conversation to anyone. If Hopkins gets there on his own, then you will be left to your own defence, sir. At present my deductions are based on conjecture with little physical evidence to prove them as fact, merely as a possible scenario, which is hardly worth reporting as it would not be enough for a court case. Consider also, Caldwell is highly unlikely to bring any matter to court that would taint the reputation of the college. Under current conditions, our accusations would fall on deaf ears.

"However, if you will trust me, I have connections with no little influence in governmental affairs. If Caldwell is as corrupt as you make him out to be, I am sure that investigations will prove that and be the ruin of him. He will not likely be put to death, unless there is some heinous act of which we are not aware, but he will be disgraced and quite likely imprisoned. A more suitable lingering punishment than a quick death, would you agree?"

"If only I could live to see it," rasped O'Hare, as another coughing fit overtook him.

"I cannot promise that," replied Holmes. "The wheels of justice often turn slowly. But even if not swift, I can guarantee they will be sure."

The gentleman stood and shook the detective's hand, "Then I will take you at your word, Mr. Holmes. Frankly, I'm not sure I have the strength for another confrontation, so I will leave it in your capable hands."

Chapter Eight

O'Hare's rapidly declining health, with its increasingly violent coughing fits, served to eliminate him from even crossing Hopkins' mind as a possible participant in the two deaths. Holmes steered the Inspector away from consideration of other suspects, citing insufficient evidence to make a case.

Finally, much to Hopkins' and Palmer's chagrin, the cases were left to stand as 'death by misadventure', but were not officially closed, in case more evidence came to the fore.

By the following October, Holmes and his government sources, (I suspect his brother Mycroft played no small part), had obtained enough evidence for Robert Caldwell's arrest on charges of receiving bribes. I arranged an ambulance to be present at the scene, so that Orson O'Hare could witness the coroner being hauled away in handcuffs to a police van and driven back to London to await trial.

The librarian passed away a few days later. Content in knowing that Holmes had kept his promise, his last words were a quote from Sir Francis Bacon, "Revenge triumphs over death". Caldwell was found guilty and sentenced to ten years in Newgate Prison.

It was less than six months later when Holmes and I read of the former coroner's death at the hands of another prisoner.

The justice which O'Hare had sought for Angelina had come full circle.

Postscript

As to the ghost of Sir Osbert Lansbury, there are still sightings from time to time, even though the tunnel has been sealed. While Holmes was satisfied that his case was complete, once we had the librarian's confession, I did a little more investigating on my own and found that Colm's older brother, Devon, was *not* in town on the day the sword was planted in front of O'Hare's door. There is always the possibility that, like Colm, Devon had associates who may have done the deed. I, however, having grown up with ghost stories in my Scottish youth and witnessing mysteries of the Middle East during my army days, am inclined to a more open mind than my friend, the scientifically logical, Sherlock Holmes.

'There are more things in heaven and earth, Horatio, than are dreamt of in your philosophy.'

(*Hamlet* (1.5.167-8), Hamlet to Horatio)

The Raspberry Tart

Editor's note: Due to the conservative values of the time, Dr. Watson had a hand-written note clipped to this story which read:

The following case contains some delicate explanations of medical conditions which may not be suitable for publication, yet their presence is essential to the story. I must consult with Dr. Doyle and the publisher as to how best to convey this aspect in the least offensive way.

Chapter One

It was early in our association, late in the spring of 1882, if I recall correctly, when a client came to engage my friend, the consulting detective, Sherlock Holmes. It was shortly after noon when he called at our lodgings at 221B Baker Street. He was a well-dressed gentleman, whom I would put in his mid-forties. Clean-shaven and of average build, he stood about five foot nine, with the demeanour of a man who could command a room with no need to resort to physical size.

He identified himself as Donald Ellington. Holmes introduced me as his 'trusted colleague', which gave me no small amount of pride. Once we sat down, my friend proceeded to address our guest in the manner with which I had begun to become accustomed.

"Tell me, Mr. Ellington, what brings a banker from Cox & Company to consult with me privately in my rooms rather than at your office on Charing Cross Road? Is there a problem at the bank, such that you wish to avoid publicity, or is this of a more personal nature?"

Ellington was taken aback. He leaned away from Holmes with such consternation on his face that I thought he might flee the room. After a few seconds, he took a deep breath to settle himself and replied, "It is not bank business, sir. But how could you possibly know what I am and where I work?"

"I will tell you only if you promise not to say, 'how simple'," said the detective.

Our guest agreed and Holmes explained, "You are a well-dressed gentleman, more so than a clerk. You have a bearing of command about you which is common to managers in business offices. Your waistcoat front indicates some minor wear from leaning against your desk, as you frequently do in order to process paperwork. But neither your hand nor shirt cuff reveal any ink stains from significant amounts of writing. Thus, you are performing tasks limited to reading and signing documents, common managerial duties of a banker.

"Your shoes, which are shined and brushed regularly, as evidenced by the condition of the leather, have received an unfortunate layer of dust on them this morning. It is not the common dust of dirt, such as one might receive from a walk in the park or in one's garden. It is, rather, concrete dust that is currently in abundance as city construction workers are tearing up the street for repairs along Charing Cross Road in front of Cox & Company. It has clung to your shoes and lower trouser legs.

"Finally, the time of your arrival coincides with the amount of time it would take a cab to travel from your office to our humble abode during this time of day, when many are out and about seeking their noon meal."

Ellington replied, "Your explanation does seem simple." Holmes scowled. "However, it is obviously the result of being an observant and intelligent man whose gifts are far beyond those of the average citizen. I am gratified that this is so. I need such a man who can use these talents, along with cunning and cleverness, to assist me in a family matter."

Appeased by the continuation of the banker's statement and acknowledgement of his skills, Holmes replied, "Then tell me, sir, what is your issue and what do you require of me?"

Ellington leaned forward, elbows on knees and hands folded. He spoke in low tones, almost as if he were afraid of being overheard, "I am a widower, Mr. Holmes, with only one son to carry on the family name. It's my son, Jasper, of whom I wish to speak. He has fallen head over heels in love with a tart who works as an actress at the Criterion Theatre named Judith Morrow. She is not of our class, but he doesn't care. He is blinded by her beauty as most young men are, including myself at that age. I understand his dalliance, for she is a pretty little thing, with raspberry red hair and a well-rounded figure. But he is talking marriage and I cannot allow such a union. If his mother were still alive, I believe she could talk sense to him. He was always closer to her. However, he has inherited my stubbornness and seems to have developed a rebellious streak since attending university."

Holmes replied with a frown, "What steps have you taken thus far? Have you met the young lady to establish her character and intentions?"

"No, I only went to the theatre one evening, without my son's knowledge, so I could see her for myself. She's a decent actress, but then, she's an *actress*! It will never do!"

"I see," said Holmes, "What have you told your son?"

The banker shook his head in frustration, "I've tried reasoning with him, bribing him and even threatening to send him to another school on the Continent. But he just says he would run away with her before allowing anything to separate them."

Holmes crossed his arms. "He seems quite determined. What would you have me do?"

Ellington sat up straight and responded, "I need you to look into her background. She is older than he, by two or three years I would guess. There could well have been a previous marriage, or at least other lovers. I need you to prove she is not the sweet young maiden he idolizes; that she's just a raspberry tart that may satisfy his sweet tooth but not sustain him for the life that his station allows him."

My companion sat back in his chair, tapping his fingers on the arm of it as he stared at our visitor. I was expecting him to inform Ellington that he did not deal with such cases and to take his business elsewhere. Instead, he stood and replied, "I shall look into it. I assume you do not wish me to communicate with you at the bank. What is your home address?"

Ellington stood also and handed him a card, which Holmes took, glanced at and turned his back to retreat to his chemistry table, saying over his shoulder, "I shall have something for you in the next few days. Until then do not threaten your son further or you may precipitate the very action you fear. Will he be at the theatre tonight?"

"No, I've sent him up to Liverpool on a business matter. He won't be back until the day after tomorrow at the earliest."

"Very well. Good day."

Our client seemed somewhat miffed at this abrupt dismissal. I walked him to the door and assured him that Holmes was already turning over ideas in his mind. After he nodded and left, I turned back to my friend and enquired, "What are you doing, Holmes? I've never seen you take a case like this before. It is surely beneath you and certainly no great exercise for your mind to puzzle over."

"You are correct on the first point, Watson. I would normally have dismissed such a client out of hand. There is something deeper here and, as I have no other case at the moment, I am intrigued enough to investigate further."

"What do you suspect by, 'something deeper'?"

"Donald Ellington is more than a concerned father," answered the detective. "He is an accomplished liar and that makes me want to find the real truth of this matter."

Chapter Two

"Really, Holmes? What was he lying about?" I asked.

"That is what I am determined to discover, Doctor, for it is a lie of omission. He is holding something back and it weighs significantly upon him. In the meantime, I suggest you take in the show at the Criterion tonight and see how good an actress this Miss Morrow is."

"What will you be doing?" I asked.

"I, or rather, Will Scott[1], veteran actor, shall arrive early and wander about backstage to learn what I can about the young lady."

"I did not realize your acting reputation was known beyond Henry Irving's troupe."[2]

"Actors go where the work is, Doctor. I have also worked for the Sasanoff Company and others. I know the stage door attendant, as well as the stage manager at the Criterion. I'll have no problem gaining access."

That evening I enjoyed dinner at the restaurant within the Criterion building, a structure that was less than a decade old. It brought back the memory of my meeting my friend,

---

[1] Holmes' stage name, based on his real name, William Sherlock Scott Holmes.

[2] In his latter university years and early career, Holmes supplemented his income as an actor. He occasionally acted with the troupe of Henry Irving at the Lyceum Theatre. Irving was one of the most famous English actors of the Victorian era and was the first actor to be awarded a knighthood. Holmes is also known to have worked with the lesser known Sasanoff Company.

Stamford, just a year and a half before at the Criterion Bar and the discussion that led him to introduce me to Sherlock Holmes.[1] The facility had been designed by the famous architect, Thomas Verity and included a large restaurant, dining rooms, ballroom, and galleried concert hall. I was only able to obtain a ticket in the upper gallery, for it was a popular show and nearly sold out. Fortunately, I had brought my opera glasses with me and was able to follow the performance of Miss Judith Morrow quite well.

Ellington had not exaggerated her beauty. She had a very pretty and expressive face with high cheekbones and a dazzling smile. Her figure was well-rounded with an ample bosom yet trim waist. The most striking feature of her appearance was her luxurious hair. It was long and full and fell in waves nearly to her waist. Its colour was a deep red, such as I had rarely seen. It was much like the hue of the well-ripened raspberries I had enjoyed with dinner just before the performance. That alone made her stand out among the women of the cast, even though she was not the leading lady.

I noted that she moved with grace and athleticism and was of excellent voice. From this distance there was not much else I could glean about her. I did note that several men in the audience near the stage, especially those close to her age, seemed quite taken with her and were especially enthusiastic with their applause when the cast took their curtain call.

I made my way backstage afterward, with the assistance of Holmes vouching for me. The usual chaos backstage during a performance had subsided. There was merely the storing of props and scenery and performers, now out of costume and makeup, bidding each other 'good night', or drifting off in cliques to some nearby pub. I was standing with Holmes when Miss Morrow's dressing room door opened. My friend had decided that would be his cue to leave and wait outside where he could catch a cab and be ready to follow her. I would exit behind her, attempting to get as close a look at her as I could

---

[1] See *A Study in Scarlet* by Arthur Conan Doyle for details of this meeting.

for signs of any medical condition she might have, or whom she might consort with.

Once out of the door however, she was inundated by a group of hopeful admirers. The crowd of young men forced her to stop and I nearly ran into her from behind. The pushing and shoving was getting out of hand. The stage door guard could not contain so many. Finally, I stepped around beside her and took her arm, using my cane to push through the chaos I called out, "Please, I'm a doctor. You must let us pass!"

That gained us enough of a pathway to make it to the street and a nearby cab. I helped her inside and reached to close the door so she could depart, but she stopped me and asked, "Are you really a doctor, sir?"

"Dr. John Watson, at your service, Miss Morrow," I replied, still attempting to close the door so she could be off before the crowd changed its mind and came after her.

"Would you please come with me?" she implored. "I have need of a doctor at home."

The crowd was starting to suspect something was up and began making its way toward us. I made the decision to jump in and join her as she called out an address to the driver. Holmes, no doubt, would not be happy that I had given away my identity.

As we rode along, I enquired as to what health condition I might be treating. She replied, "It's my mother, Doctor. She's been suffering pains in her breast and our local doctor says there's nothing to be done. I may be grasping at straws, but I'm hoping you can find something to give her some relief besides the laudanum he's prescribed."

I sympathized with her, for she seemed sincerely grieved over her mother. "I'll certainly see her, but I don't have my medical bag. It will have to be a cursory examination."

She put her delicate hand on my forearm and gazed upon me with golden brown eyes, "Whatever you can do, sir, 'twill be of some comfort I'm sure."

Weaving our way westward for about four miles, we disembarked in Chelsea on a street called Mulberry Walk. She led me to a first floor flat. Her mother was in bed asleep. It was late, being about an hour after Miss Morrow's show had ended and I whispered to her, "I hate to disturb such a peaceful repose, perhaps I should come back in the morning."

"Oh, it's quite all right, Doctor. She always wants me to wake her when I get home so she can hear how the show went. She was an actress herself and it's still in her blood."

I waited out in the hallway so as not to startle the woman, as her daughter gently woke her.

"Mum, I'm home," she spoke softly, as she laid a hand on her mother's shoulder.

The bed-ridden lady, who I would have put in her late forties, slowly opened her eyes and smiled in recognition of her child as I ducked back out of sight.

"Judy, my sweet," she said, as she reached up and stroked her daughter's hair. "How was the show? How were your curtain calls?"

"Everything went perfectly, Mum. It was a grand audience."

"Very good, very good," she replied, as her hand collapsed back onto the bed.

"Mum, I've brought a man with me who was at the show. He's a doctor. I'd like you to let him see you."

"Oh, dear, not like this! My hair! I've no makeup on. No, no child. Have him come back tomorrow."

"Mum please. He's here now. He was very kind to me after the show. He saved me from a crowd of would-be courters. When he said he was a doctor I implored him to come see you. It will only take a few minutes.

She looked back in my direction through the open door where I was just out of her mother's sight and nodded for me to come. Hesitantly I stuck my head around the corner and waved, "Good evening, madam. I'm Dr. Watson. I don't wish to disturb you, but your daughter is quite persistent."

She looked at me, gave a little "Hmmf!" and then back up at her daughter's eyes. "Stubborn you mean. Very well, Dr. Watson. You may come in."

I stepped into the room. Miss Morrow vacated her seat so I could sit at her mother's bedside. The elder woman was quite attractive for her age. I could see where her daughter received her looks. Even the same raspberry red hair, though shorter and slightly greyed at the temples, adorned her crown. She pushed herself up into a sitting position and looked me over. "A bit young for a doctor, aren't you? How old are you, boy?"

"I'm twenty-nine, madam. May I take your pulse please?"

She gave me her wrist and continued her questions, "At what hospitals have you worked?"

"I am currently working part-time at St. Bartholomew's. Prior to that I was attached to her Majesty's Fifth Northumberland Fusiliers in Afghanistan."

"An Army doctor! Have you any experience at all with female patients?"

"Part of my duties were to help treat the local populace. I've delivered children, dealt with infections and ... other female problems. At Bart's my duties include both genders and all ages ... your pulse could be stronger. What symptoms are you experiencing?"

"Judy didn't tell you?"

Her daughter spoke up, "I didn't want to prejudice his opinion, Mum. Let him determine for himself, if it's true."

I turned to the girl, "You know what's wrong?" I said, almost accusingly.

The mother grabbed my elbow and turned me back toward her, "We know what other doctors have said. Judy just won't accept it."

I nodded, then continued, "As I explained to your daughter, I was there to enjoy the show. I don't have my medical bag with me, so this examination will depend largely upon your answering questions."

"You saw the show? Wasn't she marvellous?"

I smiled, "She was indeed very fine. In some ways she outshone the leading lady."

"That's my baby! She'll be a great star, just you wait and see. She's already better than I ever was."

"Oh, Mum, that's not true."

"Yes, it is, and don't you ever doubt it, young lady!"

113

"If I may, Mrs. Morrow," I interrupted. "Please tell me what your symptoms are."

The mother took a deep breath, which made her give a slight wince, then answered. "A few months ago, I began to get a rash just here," she held her hand on her heart. "I thought it was just prickly heat or something, but then I began to get a slight discharge that was yellowish in colour. I thought it may have been some form of jaundice, so I went to see a doctor and he found lumps. Well, I had had those before and they usually went away after my time of the month. This time they have not. The doctor wants to perform some new procedure invented in Russia, but I do not wish to be anyone's guinea pig."

Needless to say, this concerned me greatly for she had symptoms of cancer. I asked her, "Does he want to do a biopsy?"

"Yes, that's what he called it. He wants me to see a Dr. William Talmadge at Charing Cross Hospital. Says he's some sort of specialist."

I nodded, gravely, "It's not a new procedure, madam. It's been around for nearly 800 years in the Middle East.[2] I saw one performed while I was over there. They don't call it that though. A Frenchman[3] gave the name to the procedure just a few years ago, after learning of Russian doctors practicing the technique.

"If your doctor is recommending this, you really must consider it. From the symptoms you've described there's a chance that you have a cancer. If that proves to be the case, delaying treatment could be fatal. Talmadge has a good reputation. I'd certainly recommend him as well"

"Just what would he do to me, Dr. Watson?"

Her concern was evident now that I had confirmed my colleague's diagnosis and I attempted to be a gentle as I could with the truth. "He will use a syringe to extract material from inside the lump so that he may examine it under a microscope.

---

[2] The Arab physician Abulcasis,(1015-1107) developed early diagnostic biopsies using needles to puncture goiters and then examining the extracted material.
[3] Ernest Besnier, Dermatologist in 1879.

He will do some tests to determine if cancer cells are present. I presume your doctor has already tested the discharge?"

"Yes, that's what made him suggest this new test," she replied. Then she reached out and took my wrist in her hand, "Tell me the truth, Doctor. Do I really have a cancer?"

"Without the biopsy, it is difficult to be sure. Unfortunately, by the time devastating symptoms present themselves it is often too late. That's why I strongly recommend you get this done immediately."

She pulled her arm back and folded her hands together in her lap as she looked down. With her head bowed, she quietly asked, "If I do have it, can anything be done?"

I sat up a little straighter, looked back at her daughter and then to her. "I'm afraid there is no cure. If it hasn't spread too far it could be removed surgically. If it is advanced your doctor can give you something to help with the pain, but there is no treatment."

She looked to the ceiling, almost as if in supplication to God. I could not let that statement hang in the air, so I continued, "Remember, Mrs. Morrow, nothing has been determined yet. There could be multiple causes for your symptoms. Even if it is cancer, you may have caught it in time. You must not give up hope. Let Dr. Talmadge do the tests and let's see where you stand."

She patted my forearm again and said, "Thank you, Doctor. I will consider your advice. I'm feeling very tired and I'm afraid I must bid you good night."

I stood, bowed to her and left the room in the company of Judith. As we walked through the flat, I noted a table with what appeared to be family portraits. I stopped to take a closer look at the man in the photos, next to a much younger version of her mother and asked, "Is this your father?"

"Yes, Thomas Morrow. He passed on two years ago. If he were only alive, I'm sure he could have convinced mother to see a doctor months ago."

"I am sorry," I said with genuine feeling. This girl hardly seemed like the sort of woman that Ellington had described. "He appears to be fairly young. How did he die, if I may ask?"

She folded one arm across her breast and held her other hand to her mouth. I immediately regretted my enquiry as it was obviously painful to her. She bore up though and answered, "Lung cancer, Doctor. Which is why I am so afraid for mum. She lived through it with him and I am not sure she would allow herself to go through with that much suffering on her own."

I placed my hand on her arm in a gesture meant to comfort, but before I could offer my condolences, she fell sobbing into my arms. Embarrassed and unsure what to do, I held her lightly and patted her back. Anything I could say would sound like a platitude. However, all I could think of was to keep her chin up and take things one day at a time until we knew for certain her mother's condition. I offered her my handkerchief as she withdrew from our embrace. She dabbed her eyes and handed it back.

"I'm sorry, Doctor. My emotions tend to run on the surface after a show and I couldn't hold back any more. Please forgive me."

"Nothing to forgive, Miss Morrow, I assure you. Anyone in your position has a right to a few tears."

She smiled, "Thank you, Dr. Watson. I shall see that Mum takes your advice."

We walked to the door, opened it and stepped out onto the stoop. She asked a question, "If we should need you again, where can we contact you?"

My Baker Street address immediately popped to mind. Then I realized that Holmes may not wish to chance her showing up there and running into him or our client. Therefore, I answered, "A message can always reach me through Bart's hospital. I'm usually there or making rounds of patient's homes."

"When you're not at the theatre," she challenged.

"A rare occurrence, I assure you." Thinking of Holmes and our mission I asked one more question. "Do you have anyone who can assist you? A beau of your own perhaps?"

A coquettish smile crossed her lovely face. "I do have a young man in my life, Dr. Watson. Although we have not reached a stage in our relationship where I have introduced him to mother in her current condition. Jasper is out of town for a few days. That's why I was so glad you came to my rescue tonight. You were a Godsend, sir."

She leaned over, kissed my cheek and said 'goodnight'.

I reached up and touched my cheek, "A lucky man, your Jasper. Does your mother approve of this fellow?"

She held the door as she leaned her raspberry tresses against the frame with a dreamy look in her eye. "She only knows what I have told her of 'my Jasper'. He is such a gentleman. I cannot imagine she would not love him on sight."

I smiled at her until she closed the door, then turned to the street wondering how difficult it would be to find a cab at that hour, which was now approaching midnight.

I needn't have worried. I hadn't walked more than fifty feet when a hansom rattled up and Holmes bade me to get in.

Chapter Three

I settled myself in beside the detective, who ordered the driver to Baker Street while I arranged traveling rugs over my legs against the night's chill. Once bundled, he questioned me. "You seem to have ingrained yourself with Miss Morrow, Watson. Is she that fickle a lover?"

I returned his jibe with indignation, "Certainly not! She was merely overwrought with emotion." I went on to explain the circumstances regarding her mother and that she considered Jasper Ellington the 'man in her life'.

Holmes stroked his chin and asked, "You say she resembles her mother, how closely?"

I thought back to the woman I met and tried to compare her to her daughter. "I would say that at her daughter's age they would have been enough alike to be sisters, but not twins. The eyes, nose and cheekbones are similar, but the mouth is slightly different. The daughter's lips are fuller. I could not see Miss Morrow's ears, as you recall her hair covered them. The hair is the exact same colour and, I would wager, completely natural."

"How young was Miss Morrow in the picture with her mother and father?"

"I did not pry so deeply, Holmes," I admonished. "I had just had to relay the news that her mother may have a terminal disease, it was hardly the time for socializing."

"I realize that, Watson, but for my own curiosity, how young was she in these family photographs?"

I tried to picture the photos on the table and could only recall one of her with her parents, "I would say she was about age three."

Holmes sat back and nodded to himself. He did not say another word. When we arrived at Baker Street, he suggested I go to bed, as he was 'going to smoke a pipe or two' while he considered the facts at hand thus far.

The next morning, I awoke to an empty flat, Holmes having left quite early according to our landlady, Mrs. Hudson. "Oh, he was off like a shot this morning, Doctor. No breakfast, not even tea. Can I get you anything?"

"Tea and toast with jam, if convenient. I have rounds at Bart's."

Thus fortified, I went about my morning duties at the hospital. I could not help thinking about Mrs. Morrow's condition. I consulted a colleague about my initial findings. He concurred my diagnosis, limited as the conditions were, was likely accurate. He also assured me that Dr. Talmadge was one of the best oncologists in London. If anything could be done, he was the man for it.

Somewhat reassured, I finished my rounds and was back at Baker Street by three o'clock. Holmes had returned and was reading over one of his indexes. "Ah, Watson! Just the man I need. Are you free this evening?"

"I have no plans. Is this for your case?"

"*Our* case, dear boy. You are playing an integral part. I find it essential that you introduce me to Miss Morrow ... as *Will Scott*, of course."

"Of course," I replied, sarcastically, as if I understood his methods.

"Patience, dear Doctor. I have been poring over files at newspaper offices all day. I have ascertained just who Miss Morrow's mother is."

"How does that help your case for Ellington?"

"A case may turn on the slightest piece of information. One must learn as much as possible about suspects, victims and even clients, if one is to arrive at the truth and a successful resolution."

"You consider Mrs. Morrow a suspect?" I asked with some indignation.

Holmes shook his head, "Our *client* considers her daughter a suspect. I believe the relationship between mother and daughter could prove revealing. Based upon your observations, coloured as they may be by your gentlemanly manners and inherent capacity to see the good in people, there may be a factor helpful to our case. It may not be likely, but it must be eliminated. Then I can re-direct my thoughts and hypotheses, if need be."

We decided I would introduce him to Miss Morrow that evening backstage. I advised him a confrontational meeting with her mother should not take place late at night, after the show, when she would be at her weakest. He, surprisingly, concurred. He suggested that we seek permission for him to visit the next day.

That evening, after the show, Miss Morrow was in her dressing room. I knocked and when she said, "Come in" I opened the door, "Miss Morrow, good evening."

She turned and smiled with recognition, "Why, Dr. Watson, good evening. So, you managed to tear yourself away from your patients for a second performance. Should I be flattered, or is there someone else attracting the attention of a handsome man like you?"

I felt a flush begin to climb my neck, because I *was* attracted to her. I subdued my natural desire however and replied, "Your charms and beauty are worth twice the price of admission, my dear. Although I know you are spoken for. I am not some masher with dubious intent. I wished to check with you about your mother and also to introduce my friend here, Mr. Will Scott. He is an actor and believes he may know her."

Holmes bowed in his most courteous fashion as he took her extended hand, "A pleasure, Miss Morrow. The doctor and I share a flat. He happened to mention he escorted you home last night and met your mother. When he described her as having the same lovely raspberry red hair as yourself, I wondered if she might be Edith Morningstar, with whom I worked in Henry Irving's production of *Hamlet* back in '74."

Her face lit up with a broad smile, "Why, yes, Mr. Scott. She was the understudy for the role of Gertrude. She rarely got to play the part and was primarily relegated to background scenes. I thought she was outstanding whenever I got to watch from the wings."

"I knew it!" cried Holmes, excitedly. "I played Rosencrantz in that same production! We never had scenes together, but your mother's beauty made her a standout, just like you are now."

Miss Morrow bowed her head in that coquettish fashion of hers and batted her eyes, "Why, thank you, sir. Are you in anything now?"

Holmes shook his head, "Sadly, no. I've been visiting some of my old haunts like the Criterion here, attempting to learn of anything new I might get in on. However, the Doctor, in spite of being the soul of discretion, let enough slip that I believed your mother to be ill. I was wondering if I might pay a call to give her my good wishes?"

"I think she would like that. Unfortunately, thanks to you, Doctor," she said, nodding my direction, "she has allowed herself to be admitted to Charing Cross Hospital for the tests Dr. Talmadge has recommended. I expect she will be there for a few days."

Holmes allowed himself a measure of disappointment. Though I knew this was not convenient to his plans and he probably felt it keener than he let on. "Oh, no, Miss. I do hope it is nothing too serious!"

He turned to me, "Perhaps, Watson, you could drop in and see if she would be up to a visit from a fellow thespian?"

"I'll do what I can, with your permission, of course, Miss Morrow?"

The actress smiled, (such an enchanting sight), and replied, "I think that would be just the thing to lift her spirits. If it's all right with her doctor then, by all means, please do, Mr. Scott."

We offered to escort her through the crowd outside to a cab and she gladly accepted. This time, however, she pulled her hair back, piled it on top of her head, covering it with a fashionable hat which had a veil to hide her face. Holmes seemed to take an intense interest in this and I made a mental note to ask him about it later.

Once she was safely off, Holmes and I retired to Baker Street. I asked him about his close scrutiny when she pulled her hair back.

"Just a small detail that may help complete the picture, Watson. A more revealing portrait of the lady's features may or may not assist our investigation. I will know more after I've met the mother. Can you get me into Charing Cross tomorrow, preferably in the afternoon, when her daughter will be performing in the matinee?"

"I don't see a problem, Holmes," I responded. "I know several doctors who work at both there and Bart's. I should be able to get you in to see her, as long as her doctor allows visitors."

"Excellent, then I propose a good night's sleep and a hearty breakfast. I intend to call on Mr. Ellington at home tomorrow and see if I can meet Jasper."

"I was under the impression that he did not want his son to know of your investigation, Holmes."

"And he shan't. I shall be in disguise and pretend to drop in on bank business. I need to see the young man for myself."

An early morning telegram informed Ellington of Holmes' intentions. The banker's reply suggested he drop in at noon, while father and son were dining. Holmes later relayed to me what occurred.

He arrived as scheduled and was shown to the dining room by the butler. The senior Ellington stood and greeted him warmly, as though he was a valued client. He then introduced his son. Jasper stood and shook Holmes' hand cordially. He suggested to his father that he leave them to their business, as he had work to do. The father frowned, knowing he was likely on his way to see his young lady in her matinee performance. Reluctantly he allowed the boy to go. He and Holmes carried on their charade and walked to the study to discuss business. Once settled and the boy was gone, our client questioned the detective. "What have you found, Mr. Holmes? Is she the little tart I suspect?"

Holmes, notorious for not revealing his thoughts too soon, put Ellington off, "My investigation is on-going, sir. Thus far, the young lady has proven loyal to your son in his absence, in spite of temptations put into her path. At present, she is more concerned about her mother's health than any intrigue you suspect."

"Her mother?" responded the banker, with some surprise. "I would have assumed her to be an orphan." He paused a moment in thought, then continued, "What self-respecting parent allows their daughter to enter the theatrical profession?"

"Life's circumstances summon strange dictations to our paths, Mr. Ellington. Some choices are not ours to make, others come from the heart and cannot be ignored. I suggest you consider your own choices of your youth and contemplate where you might have gone, had you taken another path that presented itself. It may give you a better understanding of your son."

Ellington seemed taken aback by the remark. Seizing the silence, Holmes arose, bid his client 'good day' and promised a full report soon.

By one-thirty Holmes had doffed his disguise. He retrieved me from Baker Street to journey on to Charing Cross Hospital. I was able to gain permission from Dr. Talmadge to see the lady. The cancer specialist also thanked me for my efforts in recommending seeking his opinion of Mrs. Morrow's condition. We were shown to her room and I introduced my companion as Will Scott.

She held out her hand and Holmes took it gently as he sat in a chair by her bedside, "Good afternoon, Miss Morningstar. I don't expect you to remember me, but we were in Irving's *Hamlet* together, some eight years ago."

She peered closely at him and finally nodded in recognition, "Of course, Willy Scott. How could I forget those steely grey eyes? Rosencrantz, wasn't it?"

"I am flattered at your memory, madam," said Holmes in all earnestness. "When the doctor mentioned his encounter with your daughter and described that delightful red hair, I knew it must have come from you. I am sorry to see you in these circumstances. Is there anything I can do for you?"

"Oh, that's very kind of you, Willy, but I'm afraid it's all in the doctor's hands now ... and God's, of course."

Holmes nodded, "I understand. I hear that you lost your husband a few years ago. I don't wish to be indelicate, but if there is anything I can do financially, I have access to funds that may be put at your disposal."

"Oh, Willy, that's kind of you, but why would you even think of me in such a fashion? Our camaraderie was so brief and so long ago."

Holmes smiled, and I believed he now spoke from the heart, "I never told you what an inspiration you were to me, Miss Morningstar. To see you carry on in that understudy role, so close and yet so far from realizing your goal to be the leading lady. It kept me going in my darkest hours when I thought of giving up the stage. If I can repay you for that, I would be honoured."

"You are still acting, Willy?"

Holmes actually gave a little chuckle, "Nothing Shakespearean. However, I have played some significant roles these last few years."

She smiled and replied, "Good for you! As to finances, I have some small income from my late husband's investments and Judy brings home a fair amount. Thank you for your kindness!"

During this last statement, Dr. Talmadge had rejoined us. He suggested Mrs. Morrow needed her rest. We bid her 'goodbye', walking out with the doctor.

"I could not help but overhear that last statement, gentlemen," Talmadge said. "So far her test results are not good. Any treatment option is going to be more expensive than I believe she realizes. If you can obtain funds for her, it will be of significant assistance."

Holmes nodded, "Understood, Doctor. I believe I have a source that should cover her bills. I will let you know."

Holmes insisted on sending me back to Baker Street on my own, as he had, 'a little side stop to make'.

Chapter Four

When Holmes arrived back at our flat to join me for the dinner Mrs. Hudson had laid out, I queried him on his other business that day. He merely stated it was additional confirmation of his deductions. He would reveal all at the proper time. He only needed to discern how to approach the matter. He dug into his meal heartily, which told me the case was solved in his mind. He could, therefore, afford the minor distraction of digestion.

When we finished our meal, we took up our chairs by the fireplace with brandy and cigars. I was full of curiosity about the case. However, knowing Holmes' flair for the dramatic, and that he would share his thoughts with me in his own good time, I settled down with a medical journal. He took up an evening paper as he sat across from me in his basket chair. After several minutes, he suddenly folded the paper and tossed it on to the side table next to him.

"Very well, Watson, I cannot stand to see you suffer so and your opinion may be of value to me."

I looked up from my journal at this interruption to my thoughts and replied, "Whatever are you talking about, Holmes?"

"Your curiosity over this case is practically filling the room with its aura, Doctor. You have not turned a page for over four minutes, your foot is twitching like a dancer before a performance and your eyes have been glazed over in thought.

Let me tell you what I now know and my plan for its divulging. Perhaps, with your more emotional approach to life, you may have an option I have not considered."

Flabbergasted by his analysis of my mood, I set the magazine aside and gave him my full attention. What he had to tell me was both surprising and disturbing. When I pressed him for proof, he waved my question aside and merely said, "Later, Doctor. Let me present you with the options I have considered for revelation."

After he explained his considerations and the pros and cons of each, I made a few observations, but agreed that his chosen course of action seemed the most prudent. He suggested, tomorrow being Sunday, that we should exercise that option in the afternoon. He enquired if I would be amenable to accompanying him. I insisted that he could not keep me away, as my presence may be needed. He seemed pleased by my reaction, thus he stepped out to send a telegram to Mr. Ellington, advising him of his need to join us in a meeting that would resolve his son's situation.

The following afternoon, Ellington's carriage arrived at our door. It was a modest brougham pulled by a neat pair of bays, certainly not ostentatious, yet still a symbol of moderate means. We greeted him at our front door and Holmes informed him of our need to meet elsewhere. When he told the driver where to go, it caught our client off-guard and he questioned Holmes' temerity.

"I assure you, Mr. Ellington, the person we are going to meet is essential to the resolution of your case."

Within twenty minutes we were entering the room of Judith Morrow's mother at Charing Cross Hospital. Holmes had sent word ahead to Talmadge to have her prepared to expect visitors. He was reluctant, due to her delicate state, however, when Holmes explained the matter, he agreed. Thus, the lady was ready for our visit, but not necessarily our client.

When we walked in, Holmes greeted her with an assuring warmth I had only seen on rare occasions as he sat next to her, "Mrs. Morrow, I see you are feeling a little better. There is more colour to your cheeks."

She nodded in agreement, but then she saw our client. She could not take her eyes off him, as her colour began to drain. Holmes bowed his head, "I see you have noted our companion. I must make a confession to you, madam. When you knew me, Will Scott was my stage name. I am really Sherlock Holmes. My current profession is as a private consulting detective. This gentleman is my client, whom I believe you once knew."

He turned to the banker and said, "Mr. Ellington, this is the widow, Mrs. Thomas Morrow, formerly the actress, Edith Morningstar. She is Judith's mother."

Turning back to the woman sitting up in her bed, he solemnly stated, "Mr. Ellington is Jasper's father."

Her hand flew to her mouth as she whispered, "No, no! It cannot be! Please tell me there's a mistake! Dr. Watson, this can't be true!"

I came closer and confirmed, "I'm afraid so." I looked back at Ellington. He was frozen in shock with his mouth open and hands gripping tightly onto his bowler's brim. I beckoned him forward so he could take the seat Holmes had vacated.

He slowly sat as she stared at him in disbelief. Finally, he found his voice, "Edith, I … I … I cannot believe it is really you!"

She reached up and touched his cheek with the back of her hand as she stared into his eyes, "Donald, oh my poor Donald."

"What happened to you?" he asked in quiet desperation. "You just disappeared without a trace. I searched for you for weeks. I was desperate to find you. First, I was worried, then I became angry that you had deserted me. Months went by and finally my parents convinced me to move on with my life."

"I will tell you my story, Donald, but first tell me, is it true? Are you really Jasper's father?"

"You've met Jasper?"

"Not yet, but he is all my Judith can talk about. She is sure they were meant to be together. She says she feels a connection to him stronger than anyone she's ever met. Now I know why."

The banker kept staring at her, slowly shaking his head, "I can't believe she's your daughter. When I saw her perform, and the colour of her hair, it reminded me of you and how you deserted me. It made me fear for him and what he may be getting into. That's why I was so against it. Now I understand how he fell in love with her, just as I did with you."

She took his hands in both of hers, "Donald, you must listen to me, they cannot be together. We must put a stop to it."

"What? What's wrong? They could have what you and I were denied." He pulled his hands back and suddenly was wary, "Would you have her do to him what you did to me?"

She put her face into her hands as tears began to flow, "Donald, you don't understand. Judith is your daughter!"

Holmes and I discreetly retreated to the hallway, though as a doctor I felt obliged to stay close by, should this conversation trigger an adverse physical reaction. I overheard enough to confirm what Holmes had told me the night before. When Miss Morningstar found she was with child, she knew Ellington's parents would never permit him to marry her. She left without a word and went away to an institution where she could have the child in secret. Determined not to give her baby girl over to an orphanage, she returned to the stage in Liverpool. There she met and married Thomas Morrow, a theatre manager, who adopted Judith as his own. They never told the child that Morrow was not her real father. The years went by and she later caught on with Irving at the Lyceum in London. As Judith grew, she took up the family business and her talent was now bringing her significant roles, allowing her to make a living and take care of her mother on a decent income.

Dr. Talmadge arrived shortly thereafter and we took our leave after explaining the delicacy, though not the details, of the conversation taking place within. He confided to me that Mrs. Morrow's tests indicated advanced breast cancer. She would only have a few months at best.

Holmes and I took a cab back to Baker Street in silence at this news. Upon arrival, we ensconced ourselves in front of the fire with full glasses of whisky. I do not know about my friend, but I contemplated the tragedy of happiness lost when artificial class distinction overruled matters of the heart.

Our melancholia was interrupted about an hour later, by the arrival of a message from Ellington to Holmes. My companion was staring into the fire when I answered the door and accepted the note. When I told him it was from our client he said, "I've no taste for more depressing news, Watson. You read it."

I tore it open and read as follows:

Mr. Sherlock Holmes,

Your services shall no longer be required. Please remit your invoice at your convenience. Edith and I have agreed to tell our children the truth. I have also pledged to pay her medical bills and move her and Judith into my home, where she can have a full-time nurse. I have also promised to care for Judith as the daughter I never knew for the rest of her life.

Your servant, sir

Donald Ellington

"Well, it's good to see Ellington has a heart under his banker's brain," I noted. Refilling my whisky, I asked Holmes, "Just how did you come to your conclusions? Where did you go yesterday?"

Seemingly relieved to have something else to occupy his mind, my companion put down his drink and reached for his pipe instead. Once he had it going, he replied, "You recall, Watson, from the very first I was suspicious of our client's motives. There were physical signs, twitches, the movement of his eyes and his tone of voice that led me to believe he was holding something back. I especially noted the way he said the word 'tart'. It was not delivered merely with the derision of someone speaking of a lower class. There was a vehemence there that told of a deeper story. This intrigued me and thus I took up the case.

"Your initial episode with Miss Morrow painted a far different picture of the lady from that which we had been told. It also provided me with seeds of information that needed to be nurtured. Once I met both Jasper and Judith and was able to observe their physical characteristics, I knew I had to obtain more information to confirm my theory. While Miss Morrow was performing, and her mother in hospital, I left you to stop by their home. I confess to putting my lock picks into practice, Doctor. After I had examined pictures of Thomas Morrow, I was convinced my deductions were accurate. I confirmed there were no baby pictures of Judith with Morrow. That, and my observation of her mouth and ears, which you noted were unlike her mother's, further supported my deductions. Hers are nothing like Morrow's, but they are very similar to Ellington's and identical to Jasper's. I believe it was the physical characteristics they shared that attracted them to each other in the first place. It is much like the attraction that first cousins experience. Only more so with two children who share a parent."

"Why didn't you tell Ellington all this before meeting with Mrs. Morrow?" I enquired.

Holmes shrugged, "I admit, it was a gamble, especially in exposing Mrs. Morrow to whatever reaction he might have. However, I believed that he needed to hear the truth from her own lips. As a paid consultant he could have disbelieved or ignored me. I felt morally bound to force him to confront his past and remember the feelings he once experienced, so as to better understand his son's dilemma."

"How curious," I observed, "that he should achieve his goal of ending the romance between his son and the 'raspberry tart', as he called her and instead end up with a daughter, instead of a daughter-in-law."

My friend replied, "His class prejudices led him to confront his own indiscretions, Watson. Now, he is forced to face the consequences at a price he never dreamed of. I believe it is the

Buddhists, or possibly Hindus, who have a concept for it called 'karma'."

"I am well aware of that term, Holmes," I answered. "When I served in Afghanistan, I heard it often. 'What we put into the universe will come back to us'. Much like the Bible says, 'That which you sow, you shall also reap'."

Holmes took up his glass and raised it to me. "Let us hope, dear Doctor, that the deeds you and I sow will return a more kindly crop than those of our client."

The Student Olympian

Chapter One

It was just after the New Year of 1908 that a case with international implications arose for my friend, the consulting detective, Mr. Sherlock Holmes. He had retired to his beekeeping at a little farm in Sussex some years before. I was happily married again, with a small but steady medical practice in London.

On one morning, I received a telegram from an old instructor at the University of London, Professor Jameson Terrell. He stated that he wished to see me regarding an important, but private, matter and requested an appointment on the earliest evening I had available. Happily I was able to accommodate him that very day. At six o'clock sharp, he arrived at my home. My wife welcomed him warmly and took time from her dinner preparations to offer him a cup of tea, which he politely accepted as he sat in the waiting area of my consulting room. I was just finishing the notes on my last patient of the day and then was able to step out and greet him.

"Professor Terrell, how good to see you again. How have you been?"

The elderly man rose. He must have been approaching seventy years by now, but he seemed in good health and fine shape. He appeared to have shrunk over the years, or it may have just been my youthful impression of him being so much taller when I attended his classes. Now my eyes were level with the top of his head. His hair was still full and had turned snow white, as had his beard and moustache. His grip was strong as he took my hand and replied that he was fine.

"Thank you for seeing me at such short notice, Watson. I hate to perpetrate an imposition on a former student, but your reputation and connections have become well-known and I have a problem, or rather a student of mine appears to have a problem."

I had my suspicions at that statement. Still, I invited him to sit down while I sat opposite him. I then chose to clarify what I believed to be hearing. "Do you need me in a medical capacity, or is this an issue you wish me to bring before Sherlock Holmes?"

He had the good grace to bow his head and reply contritely, "I confess, it is more in Mr. Holmes' area of expertise, though the lad is claiming a medical condition which would give you an opening to investigate and see if it is worthy of Mr. Holmes' attention. In fact, there is a possibility that Mr. Mycroft Holmes may find it of interest, as it may have an international impact."

Now I was more intrigued than piqued at being used to reach my celebrated friend, the famous detective. The fact that Professor Terrell had brought up Mycroft's name also indicated an aspect of some import.

"Please, Professor, tell me what the situation is, so that I might best determine a course of action."

"As you know, because of the Mt. Vesuvius eruption, London has been chosen to replace Rome as the site of the Olympic Games this year. One of my students, Conrad Ryder, has been approached to represent Great Britain in cycling. He is a champion cyclist. He has often competed with the Polytechnic Harriers[1], finishing first or second in most of those races.

---

[1] The Regent Street Polytechnic. This institution had been created by the vision of Quintin Hogg (1845-1903), a man who believed in the education of 'mind, body and spirit'. In 1891 it became the model for applied education across London. Visiting athletes from abroad were invited to become honorary Polytechnic members and to use the sports and social facilities at 309 Regent Street.

"However, in spite of an invitation from the British Olympic committee, approved by King Edward himself, the boy is requesting a medical deferment. I suppose that is less offensive than turning down such an honour outright. But I don't believe him, Watson.

"Ryder has always prided himself on his athleticism, and cycling is his best sport. I have known him for three years. He is currently showing no signs of injury that would keep him from competing. He's also becoming more withdrawn socially. He rarely attends any of his college activities or meetings. He used to be quite active in his club until recently. Now I've heard a rumour he has resigned. As if that weren't enough, his college work is being affected. He is in danger of failing, which would jeopardize his eligibility for the competition."

This last remark prompted a question from me, "Is it possible his medical condition is not physical but mental, or perhaps psychological?"

The Professor sat back in his chair and slowly nodded his head in thought, "I had not considered that. I am not a proponent of Freud and all these recent upstarts with their psychological falderal, but a medical condition affecting the brain could be worth considering. Would you be willing to talk to him, Watson?"

I shrugged my shoulders, "If he won't talk to you, why would he open up to me?"

"As I now sit on the admissions board as a director, as well as being a lecturer, I can order a medical examination of a student. He will be required to tell you the truth as a doctor assigned by the institute."

I shook my head, "Ever since the Kitson case[2] physicians have been wary of breaking doctor-patient confidentiality.

---

[2] The 1896 case featuring the royal *accoucheur,* Dr. William Smoult Playfair, showed the difference between lay and medical views. Playfair was consulted by Linda Kitson; he ascertained that she had been pregnant while separated from her husband. He informed his wife, a relative of Kitson's, in order that she protect herself and their daughters from moral contagion. Kitson sued, and the case gained public notoriety, with huge damages awarded against the doctor.

Even if he told me what was wrong, I may not be able to share it with you."

Terrell sighed, "I don't know what else to do. Could you at least try? Even if you can't share the actual diagnosis, perhaps you could ease my mind as to the legitimacy or the seriousness of his condition?"

Not wanting to let down my old Professor, I suggested, "Let me check with a colleague of mine at Bart's. He is a specialist in brain disorders. If he is amenable, then perhaps we can examine Mr. Ryder together."

Chapter Two

The next day I visited St. Bartholomew's hospital and consulted with Dr. Charles Steiner. He, too, was a graduate of the University of London, though a decade or so behind me. He agreed with me regarding the confidentiality issue and felt all we could do was ascertain the situation and see if we could be of some assistance to the young man.

We contacted Professor Terrell and he ordered Ryder to report to us at Bart's the following morning. I chose to stay in the background at first and take notes as a consulting physician, while Dr. Steiner took charge of the actual examination. The lad who arrived at his office was a fine specimen of athleticism. His height was about six feet and his body exhibited a lean, sinewy strength. He had short blonde hair and blue eyes that seemed to take in everything around him. His handshake was firm, though he appeared to be nervous.

"I don't understand what I am doing here," he stated as he sat on the edge of the examination table. "Professor Terrell has no need to know of my medical condition. It's none of his business."

He was trying to put up an arrogant front, but all my years of association with Holmes allowed me to read fear behind the bravado. Steiner took the lead and replied, "In his position, Professor Terrell has a responsibility for the health of his students. That includes your welfare in addition to anything contagious you might spread to others. If you have a treatable condition, he must see that you are taken care of. If you present a danger to your fellow students, he must take appropriate steps to ensure their safety as well as yours. Now, please tell us, what symptoms do you have?"

Ryder sat there, head bowed in thought as his large hands gipped the edge of the table tightly. At last he looked up and stated, "It's nothing contagious. At least I don't believe so. It's merely a sudden weakening of my right hip. Every once in a while, there's a sharp pain and my leg starts to buckle. It goes away immediately and even the residual pain of it only lasts a minute or so. But I can't cycle with it like this and accepting a spot on the Olympic team when I'm in this condition isn't fair to someone else who is being left off the team. I've cut back on my activities, hoping that less stress would allow it to heal."

Steiner looked at me behind the lad's back and cocked his head to one side in scepticism. Then he asked another question. "How do you account for the drop in your academic studies, Mr. Ryder?"

The boy sighed and replied, "I'm not an exceptional student, Doctor. I need to study very hard to keep up. Travelling to the library and ascending the steps is now painful and thus a disadvantage. Worrying about it has become even more distracting. It makes it hard to concentrate, I'm afraid."

Steiner nodded and replied, "I see. Well, let me check a few things and then I'd like Dr. Watson to examine your leg and get his opinion. He is very familiar with leg injuries.[1]"

My colleague examined Ryder's eyes, ears and even checked his sinuses for infection. He checked his throat, lymph nodes and listened to his heart and lungs with his stethoscope. Then he turned the lad over to me.

I had him lie down and felt around his hip and knee joints, pressing certain areas to determine if they were painful or numb. Then I bid him to stand next to the table and lift one foot as high as possible, then the other. First straight up, then backward and forward. I had him do slow knee bends and at

---

[1] One of Watson's war wounds in Afghanistan was to his leg.

this juncture he needed to grab the table to pull himself up as he winced in pain. I let him sit a minute. When he caught his breath, I encouraged him to walk across the room and back again while I observed if there was any leaning, foot dragging or other lack of symmetry.

Once he sat back down, I crossed my arms and said to my colleague, while keeping my eye on Ryder, "Doctor, I think we should take an X-ray of that hip, so we can get an idea of what's causing the pain. It acts like arthritis, but that would be rare in a man of his age. I'd like to rule out sclerosis or a possible fracture from bone fatigue. You haven't fallen or banged your hip lately, have you, Mr. Ryder?"

He appeared lost in thought and had to shake himself to answer, "Uh, no, Dr. Watson, nothing like that."

"Well, let's check the schedule and see when we can have this done. Perhaps even today."

Steiner offered to go and see when the X-ray machine might be available. I stayed with Ryder, whose foot was bouncing up and down with nerves. Suddenly he spoke, "Is this some bloody joke, Doctor? I thought X-rays were just a fairground trick to relieve people of their money with fake pictures of their insides."[2]

"I assure you, young man, the process is quite real. A hospital in Edinburgh has had an X-ray machine for ten years. It has been a great help in diagnosis. Doctors were even using them in the Greco-Turkish war to ensure they had found and removed all shrapnel from their patients. It will tell us if there are any deformities or things like bone spurs that could be causing your pain."

"And if you find something, you can treat it?" he asked, but not as hopefully as I would have thought.

"That will depend on what it is. Let's not speculate until we actually have a look."

When Steiner returned, he informed us that there was no opening in the diary until the following morning at ten-thirty.

---

[2] In the early days, after X-rays were discovered in 1895, fairgrounds often used them as an attraction.

We garnered young Ryders' promise to return at that time and dismissed him to go back to college.

When we were alone again, I turned to my colleague and asked, "What do you think?"

"He's definitely hiding something. The symptoms could be psychosomatic, but I believe there's a fear there of something being discovered about him that he doesn't want known."

"I agree," I stated. "His answers don't fit with his actions. It's almost like he is telling us something he's observed in others and is mimicking the symptoms. I've worked with Sherlock Holmes long enough to usually be able to tell when someone is lying and this young man definitely has a secret."

"Will you call him in on the case?" asked Steiner.

"I'll get word to him that I may require his services. He's in retirement with his bees, but perhaps this will pique his interest enough to draw him back to London temporarily."

Chapter Three

I attempted to reach Holmes by telephone that afternoon but received no answer. Therefore, I sent a telegram down to his Sussex bee farm, with what I hoped would be enough data to whet his appetite. The next morning, I had yet to receive a reply when I left for the hospital to meet Mr. Ryder for his appointment. I arrived at ten o'clock and made sure the X-ray attendants were ready to receive him.

At ten twenty-five, I was joined by Dr. Steiner and we renewed our discussion regarding our would-be Olympian. "I've had a chance to sleep on it, Watson," he began. "I'm convinced the young man has a secret. Whether it is deliberate or psychological I need to ascertain. I should like to hypnotize him. Would you be amenable to helping me talk him into that procedure?"

I was hesitant, as I had never actually witnessed this practice as a medical technique, in spite of its burgeoning popularity since the 1880s. I questioned my colleague. "I've heard of the practice, of course, but I've never seen it applied. Just what would be involved?"

He explained the procedure and the expected effects, chief being that the patients would reveal deep subconscious thoughts that may lead to what was behind their feelings or actions. I cautiously agreed, with the caveat that I be allowed to attend the session and prepare questions that I felt pertinent to be added to his own list. To this he readily acquiesced.

Having settled the matter, I checked my watch. "It may be a moot point. Our patient is fifteen minutes late. I was afraid of this. If he is, in fact, attempting the subterfuge I suspect, he knows it could not survive an X-ray examination. I will go to the University and see if he showed up today. If not, I'll get his home address and try to track him down and bring him in to see you."

The college, being less than two miles from Bart's, was a quick cab trip on this cold winter's day. The bare trees threw little shade against the sun, which shone dully through the light cloud cover. I crunched my way through the slush of day old snow until I reached the administration offices. My enquiries found that Ryder had not attended any lectures that morning. Therefore, I obtained his address and set off for his parents' home, where he lived in Lambeth. On a neat little triangle of streets called Wolcott Square, I found the correct address among the row of indistinguishable home fronts that faced the small snow-covered park and knocked upon the door.

It was soon opened by a stocky woman with shoulder length blonde hair, streaked with grey. I judged her age to be mid-to late fifties and assumed her to be Ryder's mother, as I did not expect a maid to be in service among these modest homes. Before I could introduce myself, she enquired, "Would you be Dr. Watson, sir?"

I was taken aback momentarily, then answered in the affirmative. She opened the door all the way and said, "Please, come in. You are expected, although I don't know how."

As I entered the small foyer and followed the lady, I could not help but notice, even with the voluminous beige dress which she wore, that she walked with a slight limp. It was very much akin to the symptoms her son had described and attempted to emulate, in my opinion. That thought was interrupted by the sight which greeted me in the lounge. To my amazement, there sat Sherlock Holmes! He rose upon my entrance and shook my hand in genuine affection, "Watson, old boy! It is good to see you and to see that I can still predict your train of thought. Sit down my friend. I arrived only a minute ago and was about to be regaled by Mrs. Ryder on the latest behaviour of her son."

I waited for our hostess to sit, then took a chair next to my friend. I could not get over his presence and interrogated him, "How did you come to be here, Holmes? I received no reply to my message yesterday."

"I was in town on another matter. My housekeeper relayed your message and my own deductions led me to our current location. But let us catch up later and direct our enquiries to Mrs. Ryder for now."

I spoke first and asked, "Do you know where your son is, madam? He missed his appointment at the hospital this morning."

The lady seemed genuinely surprised at my question and replied with great concern, "Why was he going to the hospital? Is there something wrong with him? Please, doctor, you must tell me!"

I glanced at my friend to see if he wished to speak. He gave a slight shake of his head, so I continued, "I don't believe there is anything wrong with him, Mrs. Ryder. He has complained of pain in his right hip. So much so, that he's quit cycling, much to the consternation of Professor Terrell. We did an examination yesterday and were going to take X-rays this morning to ascertain if there was a serious problem or not. He never arrived, so I went to the college and found that he failed to appear at his lectures today. Do you have any idea where he could be?"

"Oh, dear. He left at his normal time to go to college. He's never complained about any pain to me. As you may have observed, I am the one with severe arthritis in my hip. I did not expect it to pass on to my son so early in life. Why would his professor care about his cycling? Is there a college race coming up?"

Holmes chose that moment to answer, "Your son has been put forward to represent Great Britain in the Olympic Games next spring. It could bring great honour to both college and country if he were to compete and win a medal."

That statement seemed to freeze her momentarily. Then she asked in feigned innocence, "That would be an international competition, with other European countries?"

"Yes," confirmed Holmes, "also North and South American and Oriental athletes. He did not tell you of this?"

She took a handkerchief from her sleeve and dabbed her eyes, though I had not observed any tears during her previous concern. At last she spoke, "I'm afraid I cannot help you, gentlemen. I've no idea where he is or where he could go other than college or his club."

"We believe he has resigned from his club, madam," I answered.

She held the hand with the handkerchief to her heart and looked at me in dismay.

She then spoke softly, with distracted eyes, "Resigned from his club? I cannot believe that. All his friends, his connections for a future career …" She adopted an almost defiant stance, in sharp contrast to her previous attitude. "The club was everything to him. You must go there and find the truth, gentlemen. Perhaps one of his friends can assist you. Then you must tell me what you find. I cannot believe he would just disappear."

Holmes stood as well, and I followed suit. He addressed our hostess, "Two questions first, madam. Do you know if your son gambles?"

"I do not believe so, Mr. Holmes. He has no income for such things. My husband gives him an allowance, but it is hardly sufficient for betting."

"I see. Finally, are you aware of any young lady in your son's life? Is he courting anyone?"

"No, he has never mentioned any girl to me, and I've seen no sign of any such relationship. He keeps regular hours that would allow little time for …"

As her voice trailed off, I realized the thought had struck her that today was a perfect example of her not really knowing where her son was or what he was doing. Holmes donned his homburg and said, "Keep your hopes, Mrs. Ryder. We shall continue our search until your son is found. Come along, Doctor."

As we walked to the corner to hail a cab, I queried my friend, "I am sure if I asked how you knew I was coming here you would spout something as being 'absurdly simple', so I'll not bother. Have you any idea what is going on with this young man?"

"Only a few seeds of thought, Watson," he replied. "We shall have to sprinkle them with more data to see which ones grow into legitimate hypotheses. I would call your attention to the fine china in the lady's cabinet, especially the cups."

"I barely noticed them, Holmes," I replied. "What possible significance could they have?"

"Dear, dear Watson, all these years and you still see but do not observe," he chided.

I charged back in defence, "Once I saw you sitting there, I was taken aback. Besides, with you on the scene, what could I observe that you wouldn't?"

"*Touche'*, Watson. Just to be sure, did you observe anything about our hostess from your view as a medical man?"

I thought back to our meeting and replied, "She is right-handed and walks with a limp consistent with an arthritic right hip. While she can certainly manage around the house, I believe she uses the cane in the umbrella stand by the door whenever she goes out. Her hands exhibit the usual swelling of age, as I noted by the fact that her wedding ring's edges are overflowed by a ridge of skin tissue. She should really have it re-sized before it causes a problem. Her colour was good except when she became excited, but the redness that occurred was quite natural and no cause for alarm. She could stand to lose a few pounds, but I would not judge her obese."

"What do her blonde hair, blue eyes and accent tell you?"

I hesitated, then replied, "A blue-eyed blonde would indicate northern European ancestry. Germany or Scandinavia, most likely. But I heard no accent, Holmes."

"Merely trace elements after many years living in England. A slight trill to her R's and other pronunciations were distinctly German."

I shook my head in wonder and asked, "So, what does that tell you, Holmes?"

"At the moment, nothing. It is merely a fact to be stored and retrieved if needed to complete a theory."

Once able to obtain a cab, Holmes gave the driver the address to Ryder's club. It took me a moment, then I realized, neither I, nor Mrs. Ryder, had mentioned the name of the club. I brought this to my companion's attention. Holmes shrugged and replied, "When you mentioned he had resigned, the lady immediately glanced at a spot on the wall. I observed as we left, that it was a place where a plaque hung which had been presented to Ryder by his fellow club members for an athletic achievement. I gleaned the club name from that. Hopefully, with lunchtime approaching, we shall find members on hand who can impart more information regarding our young cyclist."

Chapter Four

We soon arrived at the Hanover Club. As Holmes had predicted, it was just after twelve noon and several men were entering the establishment, singly and in small groups of two or three. Most were young men. There were a few older businessmen as well. Being in our early fifties, Holmes and I stood out. To appear less conspicuous, I followed my friend's example and walked in with a confident air of belonging. The reception of this club was of dark panelled wood and tastefully decorated with Georgian furniture. On the walls were life-sized paintings of all the Hanoverian kings, from George I through to William IV.[1]

A young man was seated at a reception desk and Holmes approached him casually, "Excuse me, may I enquire as to whether Mr. Conrad Ryder has arrived for lunch yet?"

The fellow looked thoughtful for a moment, as if trying to remember, then replied, "I don't believe so, gentlemen, but I only came on duty at eleven-thirty. He may already be inside. Are you gentlemen members?"

I explained that I was a doctor and graduate of the University, but not a member of this particular club.

---

[1] As a woman, Queen Victoria could not legally be considered a Hanoverian ruler, though she was of that royal line. Her marriage to her cousin, Prince Albert of Saxe-Coburg and Gotha, made her son and successor, Edward VII a Saxe-Coburg ruler. To break its Germanic family roots during World War I, Edward's son, George V, officially declared the family to be henceforth known as the *House of Windsor*.

The lad answered, "As a University alumnus, Doctor, you are allowed use of the dining area, but not the rest of the facility. You are also allowed one guest, so if you wish, you may both come in for lunch. Just go down that hall, stop at the velvet ropes and turn left through the double doors."

We proceeded as indicated. Another young fellow greeted us as we entered and directed us to a table. Holmes asked, "Do you happen to know if Conrad Ryder is here?"

"No, sir. I've not seen him for a couple of days. That's not unusual. He doesn't make a daily appearance."

"We would like to get a message to him," responded the detective. "Are any of his friends about?"

The attendant looked around the dining room and pointed to a large table where three other men were seated. "Those gentlemen over there are fellows I've seen Ryder with. They're all cyclists, I believe."

Holmes thanked the lad and handed him a half crown. Then we meandered over to the table where these students were seated. My companion introduced us and enquired as to whether we might ask them about Ryder. One fellow, Richard Heinz, who seemed to be the natural leader of this clique, invited us to sit. "Why don't you join us? None of us have another lecture until two o'clock, so you can ask all the questions you like." Holmes declined the meal, much to my chagrin, and merely sat. Fortunately, a waiter arrived and offered us drinks, so I could gain at least some fortification against the chill in the air from our cab ride. I also managed to request a dessert as a small consolation to my grumbling inner man.

Holmes proceeded with his questions, "Firstly, we have heard a disturbing rumour that Mr. Ryder has resigned his club membership. Are any of you aware of that?"

The lad to my left, Aaron Kronauer by name, spoke out in surprise, "What? He's quitting the club?" The third fellow, Russell Goldschmidt, also chimed in, "I can't believe he'd abandon us completely like that. Bad enough he won't join the Olympic team, but to quit the club? That's practically treasonous!"

Holmes raised his hand and replied, "Calm yourselves, gentlemen. It is only an unconfirmed rumour, which is one of the reasons we are asking about him. Have any of you seen him, either yesterday or today?" When they all replied in the negative, he continued, "Any idea where he might be? He did not show up for morning lectures or for a medical appointment and he is not at home."

Heinz spoke up, "He's been at sixes and sevens ever since he was invited to participate in the Olympics. I don't understand why. He's a superb racer and large crowds have never bothered him. Unless he's afraid of these foreigners, but I can't believe that."

"Has he ever exhibited any strange behaviour? Perhaps going away for periods of time without explanation. Or is he courting anyone?"

All the men denied knowing of any involvement with a woman. Heinz declared, "His attendance is usually quite regular. He has taken an occasional sick day and was once down for a week with what was feared to be influenza, but it turned out to be a combination of a cold and food poisoning."

"Did any of you visit him during his convalescence and observe his illness, or was this just what he gave as an excuse when he returned?" I asked, as Holmes nodded approvingly at my question.

The men all looked at each other, shaking their heads. Goldschmidt spoke up, "I took him an assignment once, which was given on a Friday when he was sick. I never got to see him though. His mother took the paperwork from me because he was in bed resting after a feverish night. None of us saw him during that week he missed. There was fear of contagion if it turned out to be influenza."

Holmes asked, "Do you remember which week that was?"

Heinz replied with the approximate dates and the others confirmed them. Kronauer then added an interesting tidbit. "The odd thing about his other absences is that they were nearly all on a Friday or a Monday. I can only recall one that was mid-week."

"That is right," confirmed Goldschmidt. "It seemed convenient that he was getting a long weekend out of his illnesses, but we just put it down to coincidence."

I noticed the subtle shift in Holmes' demeanour at the mention of that word. A minor change to his facial expression, a tightening of the lips and narrowing of the eyes. Hardly noticeable to a stranger, but to myself, who had known him for nearly three decades, they were as plain as day. He thanked the gentlemen for their assistance and gave his card, asking that, should they hear anything, to contact him and also to let Professor Terrell know.

As we left, Holmes was deep in thought, his head bowed, staring down at the pavement, taking in nothing of his surroundings. He seemed so distracted by this mental process that I made sure I remained in his peripheral vision so that he would not wander off course and end up walking into some temporary snowdrift created by the cleaning of the pavement. I flagged down a cab. When Holmes made no effort to give the cabbie an address, I instructed him to take us to Bart's. Midway through our journey, as if awoken from a trance, Holmes looked around, recognized the surroundings and called out, "Never mind, driver. Stop here please. If you care to wait, we're going down the street to number twenty-four first. Then to Westminster, I believe."

The promise of a fare to Westminster was enough incentive to make the cabbie wait and he plodded along beside us as we walked the hundred yards or so down Montague Street to number twenty-four. It took me a moment to recognize the place. Then I realized the last time I was here was in 1881, helping Holmes to move some of his things to our newly shared flat in Baker Street.

The wrought iron railing still lined the front and up the steps to the black door with the brass number twenty-four upon it. Above the door a fantail window allowed light into the entrance porch. Holmes led the way up the steps but did not knock. He merely turned and slowly gazed up and down the street which was once so familiar to him. He closed his eyes for a moment and took a deep breath, as if he could draw some ancient memory into his mind. At last he opened his eyes and walked across the street where a telephone box now stood. He gave the cabbie a sign to wait just one more minute. After his call, he led the way back to the cab and said, "Slight change of plans, my good fellow. Please take us to the Diogenes Club."

Chapter Five

"Why the Diogenes Club, Holmes?" I asked, as the driver whipped up his pair of roans and we began our journey to the west end.

"Because I just confirmed that Mycroft is not in his government office," he replied.

"I gathered that we were going to see Mycroft, since there is no other reason to visit the Diogenes Club. But why? Professor Terrell also brought up Mycroft's name. How would the Professor know Mycroft, and what possible connection could Mycroft have to Ryder?"

"I have a theory which fits the facts as we know them, Watson. Our fortuitous happenstance upon Montague Street reminded me of my early days of detective work, before my practice began to flourish. You are aware that Mycroft abhors physical activity. He often called upon my assistance in those times when he needed 'boots on the ground', so to speak. The Professor likely only knows of Mycroft through your publications."

"Yes, of course. But what does that have to do with Ryder?"

"Think on the things we have observed. Both he and his mother are blue-eyed blondes. He is a member of the Hanover Club, the cups in their china cabinet were of distinctive origin. Also, recall the names of his closest friends."

"Richard, Aaron and Russell?" I replied

Holmes smiled and pulled his hat down over his eyes, and said just one more thing, "Think of the whole picture before us, Doctor."

Our arrival at the Diogenes Club was met with a slight delay while the attendant sought out Mycroft Holmes and obtained permission for us to meet him in the Stranger's Room, the only place in the Club where conversation was permitted. When we walked in, Mycroft was seated next to a window overlooking the street, apparently making casual observations as a matter of habit.

My companion walked over next to his brother and gazed out upon the scene. "Observing the retired Sergeant-Major taking his horse to his blacksmith, or the widowed mother taking her baby to the doctor while her elder son exhibits his reluctance to have to tag along?"

The senior Holmes answered, "I was more interested in the banker *en route* to his assignation with his mistress. He is a minor manager at an institution where certain government accounts are kept. Such a lack of trustworthiness may carry over into his profession. I shall have to keep an eye on that."

From what I could see through the window, their observations seemed unfounded. However, after witnessing this scenario over many years, I knew they each had seen slight details that revealed these stated facts, which a casual observer would find speculative at best.

As they finished their conversation and we all took to armchairs about a small table, Mycroft made one more comment, "What possessed you to stop at your old lodgings in Montague Street after you left the University, Sherlock?"

My friend seemed to take it in his stride that his brother knew our whereabouts. Then Mycroft stated, "You really must drop the matter. You realize that?"

"So, you are confirming your involvement, dear brother? I can assume national interests take precedence?"

"Indeed, he is a key cog in the machinery."

"But what of national pride? And his own competitive spirit? Must those be cast aside?

"They are not my concern. My course and goals are firm for King and Country and the greater good. Sporting events are tools to be used, not the true prizes that must be won."

My friend pondered that for a moment, while the conversation had left me far behind. However, I chose to await further discussion rather than interrupt for an explanation.

The younger brother turned to his elder, "You recall the Wagner case you threw my way in 1879 to help supplement my income?"

Mycroft cocked his leonine head at his sibling and raised an eyebrow, "You believe the boy capable of that?"

"If it is his only opportunity to be rewarded for his talent, the least we can do is put the matter before him."

Mycroft took a deep breath and let it out in a huff. He pulled a paper and pencil from his pocket and wrote a message, then turned it over and wrote an address. Handing the note over, he stated, "His mission must *not* be compromised. See to it, Sherlock."

As we got into a cab outside the club, Holmes gave the driver the address on the paper Mycroft had provided. Settling back in his seat, I could contain my curiosity no longer. "Holmes, I confess that the conversation I just witnessed may have been the most cryptic I have ever heard. I'll not bother asking about what you two were observing outside the window. I've seen that game often enough. However, after we sat down, you seemed to be speaking of Ryder, though I could make neither heads nor tail of what you were saying."

In response, Holmes handed me the message Mycroft had written. Above the address he had given the cab driver was the name 'Konrad Reinsdorf' written in Mycroft's firm hand. The back read, 'Feel free to consider Sherlock's proposal, BUT mission must remain intact. – M'. The 'M' was written in a highly stylized fashion, unlike the few samples of Mycroft's handwriting I had ever seen. I mentioned this to my companion.

Holmes glanced at it and replied, "It is a unique code which Mycroft uses to guarantee the authenticity of his signature. He incorporates ----------[1] into the letter so the recipient knows it is not a forgery."

"So is Konrad Reinsdorf Ryder's real name, or vice versa?" I asked.

"I believe it to be the name he has been assigned for his work with Mycroft. It may also quite possibly be the name he would have had, if his parents had not migrated from Germany. A key to a successful undercover identity, Watson, is to keep as close as possible to the real facts of a person's life. That way their answers sound more casual and realistic during conversations or questioning."

"So, Ryder is one of Mycroft's operatives?"

"Of course, Watson. His Germanic appearance, the culture and traditions he grew up with in his parents' house. I've no doubt he learned the language from them. That would eliminate any linguistic errors from someone who had to learn German from books or instructors. He was in the perfect position to infiltrate the Hanover Club, where pro-German sentiment runs high. His friends, whose first names you so admirably recalled, have surnames of Heinz, Kronauer and Goldschmidt, all solid German stock."

I responded, "Wasn't it only ten years ago or so, that Mycroft requested us to stop anti-German factions[2] that were conspiring against the Kaiser? Now we're spying on him?"

Holmes replied, "An ancient Chinese warrior said, 'Keep your friends close and your enemies closer', Doctor. The British Empire keeps a close watch on both. While the Queen was still alive, England could maintain cordial relations with her grandson, Kaiser Wilhelm II. Now that his cousin, King Edward, sits on the throne, we have two men who are not kindly disposed toward one another. Wilhelm's expansionist actions around the world is intended to surpass the British Empire in strength and influence. Here is our destination. This discussion of world politics shall have to wait."

---

[1] Watson deliberately left this fact blank. Obviously to protect Mycroft's secret.

[2] *The Kaiser Role* in *A Sherlock Holmes Alphabet of Cases*, Volume 3 by Roger Riccard, Baker Street Studios Limited (2019).

We paid the cabbie and ascended the front steps of a modest house squeezed into a long row of similar dwellings. Holmes instructed me to take the lead in announcing ourselves. We were pleasantly surprised when the door was answered by an agent of Mycroft's whom we both knew.

"Doctor Watson, Mr. Holmes! Please, come in."

We entered as we greeted him, "Remington,"[3] I said. "It's a pleasure to see you again."

"I echo Dr. Watson's sentiment," said Holmes, "We've come to see your charge, young Conrad."

Remington nodded and raised his voice over his shoulder, "It's all right! You can come out. It's Dr. Watson and Sherlock Holmes!"

Turning back to us he explained, "There's a secret panelled wardrobe where he is instructed to go whenever I answer the door. Just to be safe."

"A wise precaution," said the detective. "I would have expected no less from my brother."

Conrad Ryder stepped out into the entrance hall and greeted us warily. Remington waved us all toward the sitting room, where we took up seats around the fireplace. The young man has not shaved since I'd last seen him and it gave him a more mature, if dishevelled, look. Holmes handed him Mycroft's note as a preface to our conversation.

Ryder looked it over and then sceptically at my friend, "So what is this proposal you have, Mr. Holmes?"

My companion answered with a question of his own, "First, I must understand your current status with the assignment Mycroft has given you. Perhaps you should start at the beginning as to how you came to choose to work for my brother?"

The boy leaned back in his chair and smirked, "It was not my choice at all, sir. It was a role I inherited from my father."

I spoke up, "Your father was a spy?"

---

[3] James Richard Remington assisted Dr. Watson in the adventure of the *Three French Henchmen* in *Sherlock Holmes: Adventures for the Twelve Days of Christmas*; and both Holmes and Watson in the case of *The Kaiser Role*.

"Spy is such a provocative word, Doctor," he replied. "The kind that can get you shot. He was a disaffected Prussian government official who was opposed to the Franco-Prussian War. He attempted to thwart the loss of Prussian lives in a violent scheme to unite the German states. He could not risk communicating directly with France, but his duties regularly had him in contact with England at a time when the Saxe-Coburg roots of Queen Victoria still meant something. As a confidential informant, he was able to deliver information to the British Foreign Office which they could pass on to the French. As the war was coming to a close, he realized that the unification would succeed. A new administration under the Kaiser might uncover his activities. Thus, he and my mother defected to England. He changed his name from Gustav Reinsdorf to Augustus Ryder and continues to work as a translator for the British government. Somehow your brother got the idea in his head that my athletic accomplishments might be a perfect cover to travel to Germany and participate in events there. I also joined the Hanover Club to be on the lookout for German sympathizers."

"Wait," I interrupted. "As I recall at the time, popular British sentiment was in favour of Prussia against France."

Holmes chided me, "The press pushed that sentiment, Doctor. But Prime Minister Disraeli saw war as a dangerous conflagration that could spread to our own shores. He prepared England under an armed neutrality, hoping that we would not have to take sides or defend ourselves against an overconfident victor. Enough of history. Tell us, Mr. Ryder, what is your current situation?"

"You're aware that the British Olympic Organization has requested me to represent us on the Cycling team. An honour to be sure and something I would have eagerly accepted. But my situation is intolerable. I cannot chance being recognized by German athletes who have come to accept me as one of their own. If they discover I am a British citizen, my usefulness to the Foreign Office and Mr. Holmes comes to an end."

"You've been in contact with German Olympic hopefuls?" I asked.

"Worse than that, Dr. Watson. I've received a request to be an alternate on the German Olympic Cycling Team."

Holmes spoke up at that point, "So your 'illnesses' have actually been to cover your travels to Germany and insert yourself among their athletes, who would also be their soldiers should war come to Europe. Clever of my brother to conceive such a plan."

We all sat in silence, pondering this revelation. Holmes drew out a pipe and stuffed it with tobacco from his pouch. As he prepared to light it, he announced, "Let me cogitate on this momentarily, gentlemen. I have a plan which my brother and I used once before. I need to think through some details to convince myself that it can be adjusted to this scenario. Please leave me alone for the next ten minutes."

He sat back and closed his eyes as a steady stream of smoke emitted from his pipe. The rest of us adjourned to the kitchen, where we indulged in biscuits and coffee and I gained a few more details of Ryder's cycling career on both sides of the channel.

"As Konrad Reinsdorf, I've competed in several significant races in Berlin and Hanover. As I did not want to become too much of a celebrity, I held back, so as to just make a good showing and gain their respect. I would usually finish in the top three with an occasional win only if the field was weak and my holding back would be too obvious. I certainly never expected to be asked to be an alternate on their Olympic team."

I nodded, "I was a rugby player in my school days. I know the competitive spirit can run deep. I imagine it would be quite a blow to subjugate your talent to your government work."

He sighed and replied. "Certainly not a situation I relish. What I do for King and Country is important work. Information I come across could prevent a war. Giving up a chance at an Olympic medal is a small price to pay for the potential saving of thousands of lives."

"It may not come to that," came Holmes' voice from the doorway. He walked in and helped himself to a cup of coffee. "Tell me, Mr. Ryder, or actually for this question it would be

Mr. Reinsdorf, "What do you normally wear when you compete?"

The lad cocked his head at the odd question then raised his eyebrows and replied, "Shorts, a long-sleeved, pullover shirt, rubber soled athletic shoes and thick socks."

"So, your arms have never been exposed to anyone in Germany?"

"No, sir."

"How about here, at the University?"

"Well, certainly in the gymnasium shower room."

"No common showers in Germany, then."

"No, we all went our own way after the races. I would always clean up back at my hotel."

"Very good," replied the detective. "I believe then, that I have a plan which will allow you the possibility to still compete and maintain your cover."

Holmes laid out his idea. Remington, the long-serving government agent was aghast. I was sceptical, but reserved judgement. Ryder listened carefully, then questioned my friend, "Surely my close friends and teammates here would see through that, Mr. Holmes."

"If they thought to look closely enough," he agreed. "However, we are going to take steps to eliminate the thought of you from their consideration."

Chapter Six

A week later found me escorting Mr. Ryder back at the University of London where our first stop was Professor Terrell's office. My old lecturer looked up from his paperwork in great consternation when he beheld us in his doorway.

"Watson, Ryder! What is this?" He stood up and came around his desk to attend to us. Looking down upon his student in a wheelchair he asked, "What happened?"

I answered in my professional capacity, "Mr. Ryder, here, was found recuperating in the Charing Cross Hospital. He was beaten and robbed and thus had no identification on him, making him hard to locate. He was unconscious for some time. Fortunately, he has recovered from his head injury. However, the beating exacerbated the hip condition that's been bothering him and he has to have surgery. I'll be escorting him to a specialist I know at the Nuffield Hospital in Bristol, where he will have his operation and recuperate in the healing waters at Bath. He will be gone for some months and wanted to see about getting any work from his professors, so as to keep up his studies."

"Oh, my goodness! You poor boy!" cried the elderly scholar. "Of course, I'll send a memorandum around to all your lecturers to prepare a list of work for you. The library at Bristol is top drawer. You should have all the resources you need. Do you know where you'll be staying?"

Ryder hesitated and looked up at me from his wheelchair. I replied to Professor Terrell, "Arrangements are still being made. For now, anything for him should be sent to his home. His parents can forward whatever arrives after he departs."

"I'll see to it," declared my old professor. He put out his hand and shook Ryder's, "I am so sorry for your circumstances, Mr. Ryder. You have my condolences over your lost opportunity to compete in the Olympics. A sorry shame."

"Thank you, Professor. I intend to get back to cycling if my healing goes well. Perhaps 1912 will be my year."

"I hope so, lad. You take care of yourself and mind Dr. Watson here. He was one of my best students."

"I'll do that, sir. Thank you."

From there we went over to the Hanover Club. Much the same sorrow and condolences were expressed by his friends and teammates. Thus, the racing career of Conrad Ryder came to an end for the 1908 season.

*****

Some three months later, Holmes and I attended the cycling events at the Olympic Games. The White City Stadium was brand new at the time, built specifically for the games and had a capacity of 66,000. Somehow, Holmes had procured front row seats near the finish line for each of those races. The weather was poor and often the races were delayed in order to sweep away puddles which had accumulated. As the day wore on, Great Britain made an excellent showing. Gold medals in various events were won by Victor Johnson, Benjamin Jones, Clarence Kingsbury and Charles Bartlett. Jones and Charles Denny also won silver. Germany won a bronze in the 660 yard race and a silver in the Team Pursuit.

A race of special interest to us was the 1,000 yard sprint. Johnson, Jones and Kingsbury made the finals for Great Britain. Maurice Schilles represented France. The announcer closest to us also mentioned a German racer, but the pro-British crowd was cheering too loudly for us to hear. Holmes trained his binoculars on the field and, with a grunt of satisfaction, handed them to me. I focused on the starting line and noted the boy wearing German colours had long straggly blonde hair, a short beard and a full moustache. He wore a sleeveless racing shirt which exposed his arms. On one bicep was the Imperial German Eagle. This coat of arms showed a black, single-headed eagle with a red beak, tongue and talons, with the Prussian eagle on its breastplate and, above its head, the crown of Charlemagne with two intersecting arches. On his left bicep was a large German 'R' with 'Reinsdorf' on a ribbon beneath. I handed back the binoculars to my companion with a smile, but also a question, which he stopped me from asking as the race was about to start.

The track was quite sloppy with mud and certainly no records were expected to be broken. The gun sounded and they were off. Soon though, Johnson suffered a punctured wheel and retired. The other riders crawled around the track, jockeying for position on the soft turf. Having gone through several heats to get to this point, the finalists were all top-notch racers and the lead changed several times. When the final sprint occurred on the last lap, Kingsbury also punctured a tyre as he entered the main straight. Jones, Schilles and Reinsdorf were neck and neck down the stretch. With roughly 30 yards to go, Reinsdorf was in the lead by a half-length. Then disaster struck. The chain on Reinsdorf's wheel snapped. With no more resistance to his furious pedalling, the boy was thrown off balance and went down. The other riders flew past. Jones and Schilles raced to the finish line, with Schilles winning by mere inches. However, the race took longer than the 1 minute 45 second time limit and was declared void by the Olympic ruling committee. Therefore, no medals were awarded for that event.

As Reinsdorf slowly wheeled his damaged bicycle toward his waiting German teammates, he happened to glance in our direction. In spite of his defeat, he managed a quick smile and a nod toward us. Win or lose, he had been given his chance after all.

After Holmes and I retired to a nearby restaurant for dinner, I was able to put my question to him. "How will Ryder explain those tattoos when he returns to his own teammates, Holmes?

Surely, they will recognize them and realize he raced for Germany against his own country. He's bound to be ostracized for that. I thought he was just going to use the longer hair and beard to hide his identity, as you said you were able to do in the Wagner case for Mycroft."

Holmes took a sip of wine and replied, "In my travels as Sigerson[1] throughout India and the Far East, I came across the practice of Henna tattoos as a form of body decoration. These are not permanent creations as are those done by the needle of the traditional tattoo artist. They are, instead, drawn on with ink and fade or can be easily be washed off with olive oil. His British mates will never see them. He will also cut his hair and shave before he returns to University. His explanation to his German cohorts has been that he chose to grow out his hair and beard to present a more intimidating look to athletes from other countries. The tattoos were his expression of German pride for this occasion. Thus, he maintains his identity on both sides of the channel."

"Well done, old chap!" I declared. "Plus, he got to prove he was among the best in the world at his sport. That must be satisfying in its own right."

Holmes nodded and reflected, "If only the nations of the world could set aside their petty political agendas and come together in the spirit of sportsmanship in all things."

He raised his glass in salute and I joined as he toasted, "May the Olympic Spirit continue to stir men's hearts to their better natures."

---

[1] Holmes' alias during his three years in hiding from Moriarty's gang after the Reichenbach Falls incident. See Doyle's submission of Watson's story in *The Adventure of the Empty House.*

Death on the Thames

Chapter One

What few leaves left on the trees were a wide variety of reds, yellows and oranges that threw little shade against the bright, but heatless, autumn sun. I crunched my way through their crisp, brown comrades that littered the pavements, until I reached the steps of 221B Baker Street. I was returning from a long night with a sick patient whose fever had finally broken with the dawn.

When I arrived, there was a gentleman on our steps just reaching for the bell. I was surprised at so early morning a visitor and called up to him, "Hello, sir. May I help you?"

"Is this the residence of Mr. Sherlock Holmes?"

"Yes, indeed. I am Dr. John Watson. I share these lodgings with Mr. Holmes. May I have your name?"

The fellow stood up straight and announced himself with formality, "Inspector Carmichael, Thames River Police."

He was a stout fellow, built like a rugby player with a thick body and large hands. He was about my height and looked to be in his mid-thirties. A full black moustache was the only adornment to his face, which was squarely built with firm jaw and keen brown eyes which had a look of anxiety about them.

I smiled, hoping to put him at ease, "Let me show you up to our rooms, Inspector. I'm sure Mr. Holmes will welcome your visit."

"Thank you, Doctor. It is rather urgent."

I took out my key and let us in, then led the way upstairs. During our ascent I was hoping the gentleman was bringing an interesting case to my friend. Business had been slow of late and I feared Holmes' complaints about the lack of originality among the city's criminal classes would lead him to the cocaine bottle. We had only been living together since January, but even these ten months had been enough for me to beware his mood swings when his mind was not sufficiently exercised.

Upon entrance to our sitting rooms, we found my fellow lodger in his mouse-coloured dressing gown, hair still messy from sleep. His eyes, though, were tightly focused on the morning papers, seeking some stimulus for his brain. Seeing we had a visitor, he cast the papers to one side and approached us anxiously.

I introduced the Inspector as Holmes shook his hand and then bid him sit on the sofa. I offered the fellow some tea and attempted to take his hat and coat, but he declined. Holmes remarked, "Tea won't do, Watson. This man needs a stronger dose of caffeine after a long night, as do you, I perceive. Perhaps some black coffee, Inspector?"

Carmichael seemed a bit taken aback, but replied, "Yes, you're right. Some coffee would be most welcome."

I took that as a cue to call down to our landlady, Mrs. Hudson, for a fresh pot. I then sat on the opposite end of the sofa from our guest, "What has kept you up, sir? Surely you are not ill?"

"If only that were my excuse, Dr. Watson, I would be much more the glad for it."

"Don't be droll, Watson," interjected Holmes. "The Inspector has obviously been on a case that has kept him from his wife and daughter all through the night." Addressing our guest, he continued, "From your countenance and demeanour, I would venture you have a murder victim on your hands and not an ordinary one."

Mrs. Hudson arrived at that moment with a fresh pot of coffee and three cups. I poured one each for the Inspector and myself, but Holmes declined. Taking a healthy swig, Carmichael answered Holmes' question, "Inspector Gregson warned me of your unique deductive ability. You obviously noted my wedding ring, but how did you discern I had a daughter?"

Holmes waved away the question impatiently, "There are two strands of curly blond hair caught in the pocket flap of your coat. It is remarkable that they are still in place, as you have not had a chance to go home and change since you left for work yesterday morning. Your eyes and clothes betray your sleepless night and were the case ordinary, you would not seek my assistance. Now, tell me all and leave out no detail. Watson, be good enough to take notes."

I retrieved paper and pencil from the writing desk and prepared to record our conversation. Carmichael fortified himself with another gulp of coffee and set his cup on the table. He pulled a notepad from his breast pocket and began his tale.

"I should prefer to explain to you along the way, Mr. Holmes, for there are many folks anxious to depart the scene of the crime. However, I realize you must have a summary of facts to determine if you will take the case. To be brief, there's been a body discovered on a Royal Riverboat. It was *en route* from Kew Palace to Westminster after a late evening ball. As you can imagine, there are several members of high society aboard. When the body was discovered, the captain anchored the boat mid-stream so the culprit would be confined on board. He signalled a police launch and we began our investigation. I'm afraid we're a bit lost at the moment and there are several threats being made against me and my officers by some influential people if we don't release them. One of the cooler heads, Admiral Alston, suggested I bring you in."

Holmes, champing at the bit for a case, immediately rose and started for his bedroom, calling back as he went, "I shall be with you momentarily, Inspector. Watson, if you are amenable, I should welcome your company and that of your service revolver as well."

Carmichael and I both gulped down our coffee and I re-donned my overcoat and bowler. I also retrieved my Webley revolver from a desk drawer. Holmes emerged in less than two minutes, wearing his Inverness coat and ear-flapped traveling cap to guard against the autumn chill and river breezes.

On the cab ride to Chiswick Quay to catch a launch out to the boat, Carmichael gave us a little more detail, including one very significant fact.

"The boat departed the dock near Kew Palace around midnight. Prince Albert, Prince Arthur and Princess Beatrice chose to remain at Kew for the night. There are eight others who boarded for the journey back to Westminster where they would be conveyed to either Buckingham Palace or their own residences. In addition, there were six crew members aboard: the captain, two stokers, an engineer and two stewards. After getting underway, more wine was requested by some guests and one of the stewards went to fetch it from the cold storage room. When he opened the door, he found the body of a man whom we've yet to identify. It appears frozen stiff, Mr. Holmes."

I asked him, "Were you able to detect the cause of death?"

Carmichael cleared his throat and replied, "We have not moved it yet, Doctor, hoping to retain evidence, thus we cannot make a full examination. The coroner is standing by."

I replied, "Did Dr. Drake himself come, or did he send one of his assistants?"

"Drake is there. With a Royal vessel involved he is insisting on handling the case himself."

I turned to Holmes, "Drake is well-respected, Holmes. I've met him on two occasions at the hospital. He is quite thorough and knowledgeable."

My friend nodded, "Yes, I'm aware. I've worked with Drake before and he has been accommodating to my investigations. That will be convenient. Tell me, Inspector, what time was the body found?"

"Approximately twelve twenty-five."

Holmes stroked his chin, "Interesting. I would submit to you that the murder could not have been committed after leaving Kew Palace *if* the body was, indeed, frozen stiff. Did any of these passengers take the ship from Westminster to Kew for the beginning of the ball?"

"All of them, Mr. Holmes. In addition, the Royals who remained for the night and some of their servants."

My friend nodded, "You may need to cast your net wider than you thought. We'll have to see what Dr. Drake has to say."

Chapter Two

We took a launch out to the boat, anchored mid-river off the Chiswick Quay. The early morning sun glared off the windows and brass fittings. It was gleaming white with polished teak wood cabin and accents. It had its engines idling to maintain comfort for the passengers and to be able to get underway as soon as the police allowed.

We boarded and were introduced to Captain Hunt. He was a middle-aged man with short cropped brown hair under his uniform cap. He bore a full beard and moustache to protect against the cold winds common to sea life. His heavy pea coat could not hide his athletic build and his manner was strictly military as he welcomed us aboard.

"Welcome back, Inspector," he bellowed against the sound of the engines, "I hope you brought us a saviour from this hodgepodge of lords and ladies. They're threatening everything from court martial to flogging for me and my crew. Not to mention you and your men. Of course, they are a bit into their cups and several have nodded off. Dr. Drake is with the body."

We descended to the galley and the cold storage room where we found the good doctor. Drake must have been nearing seventy by now, his Scots burr heavy in the moment, indicating the stress he was feeling. He was short and stocky, his once brown hair now nearly completely grey, yet still luxuriant. His face was clean-shaven, graced only by the gold-rimmed glasses that augmented his hazel eyes. He was kneeling by the body, attempting to manoeuvre it for better visibility but the stiffness of the limbs and dead weight were working against him. He looked up at our approach.

"Sherlock, Dr. Watson! Thank goodness you've come. I need someone who understands the importance of retaining medical evidence to assist me. Come, take a look for yourselves."

He stepped aside and we moved to either side of the body. I noted the rigidity of the limbs and the blueish hue to the skin. It was a young man, likely in his late twenties. He was well dressed, though not formally for the ball. He had dark, wavy hair and a military moustache. There was an overcoat, but no hat, and a well-tailored dark blue suit and tie.

My companion felt around the fellow's pockets but discerned no papers or other identification, he did manage to manipulate one of the victim's arms enough to pull back the fold of his coat. There was no wallet, but Holmes, did make a sound of satisfaction at something he observed. After that, he became less interested in the body and chose to examine the door frame, lock and floor. He pointed out some smears on the frosted surfaces to the Inspector, then he crouched to peer at the inside door handle with his magnifying lens. After that, he stood and declared to Carmichael, "Inspector, I suggest you advise the Captain to continue on to Westminster, but keep his speed under five knots. That will give the passengers the illusion of moving on to calm them down, yet still give us ample time for investigation. There is no need to detain all the guests at this point, for certainly this fellow was dead long before they boarded. I should like to question them now, to see if any can shed light upon this dark case."

"Easily done, Holmes," replied Carmichael. "If you'll just come with me."

Drake spoke up, "Sherlock, I haven't even determined the cause of death yet! Certainly, it's several hours ago. But, wouldn't the 'how' be prudent to know?"

"All in good time, Doctor. I'll leave the precise medical determinations to you and Watson. I'm sure you'll agree that this room is not cold enough to result in a body freezing stiff in

178

the short amount of time it could have been on board. More likely some paralytic was administered to this poor fellow and he was placed here to give the appearance of freezing, or at the very least, to effect *rigor mortis* and make it harder to determine the time of death. Right now, it is imperative that I speak to the passengers and crew while they are in this state of agitation and fatigue. It will also give me the opportunity to gain a look at their wardrobe for this evening."

He turned on his heel and left with the Inspector. I looked at the elderly physician and asked, "Now, why the deuce would he want a look at their wardrobe?"

Drake smiled and replied, "When you've known Sherlock a little longer, Dr. Watson, you'll learn that he always has a reason for what may seem the most incongruous action. I remember the first case we met, oh, it must have been 1877, or maybe '78. Anyway, he was allowed to observe as part of a group of students while I was discussing a deceased young fellow whose body had been found by the side of a road. Sherlock started at the front of the group, but after a quick look at the body, which was badly bruised and scraped from its impact with the pavement, he drifted off.

"Well, I just assumed he was a bit squeamish and chose to back away before he embarrassed himself with a nauseous reaction. I went on to explain to the group that the fellow had likely been thrown from a horse and possibly stepped upon by the creature, which would account for the bad bruising and fatal head wound. After I had finished and the group was starting to leave for its next stop, I noticed this fellow in a corner, bold as brass, examining my corpse's clothing, paying particular attention to the fellow's shoes.

"Suddenly he spoke, 'Dr. Drake, I'm afraid you are mistaken. This fellow is a cyclist and was most probably run off the road by a vehicle. Deliberately, I believe, as the driver stole his bicycle and quite probably delivered the fatal blow to the head with some type of cudgel.'"

The police surgeon smiled, "Well, of course he was right. Wear patterns on the soles of the shoes and lower trouser legs were consistent with a bicyclist. A further examination of the

179

area where the body was found showed that the pavement had been scraped by some metallic object, almost certainly the bicycle frame as it was knocked aside. It turned out his rival for a young lady's affections had run him off the road."

I nodded, "He appears to be correct in this instance as well. This room, in spite of its ice storage, could not have resulted in this man's condition."

"Oh, I quite agree and he's right, the time of death will be difficult to determine. He'll have better luck examining the passengers and crew than we will with the body."

Chapter Three

The lounge area of the craft was of extreme extravagance, befitting the royal family. Persian rugs bedecked the floor. Gold fittings adorned the cabinetry. Silver tea services and utensils abounded and the finest crystal glassware was in full use as most of the guests had been indulging in wine or other spirits.

Some of them had dozed off in their chairs, but just as Holmes and Carmichael entered the room, the sound of the engines increased and the boat began to move again. This stirred the drowsier passengers and the sight of Carmichael attracted everyone's attention.

Before they could start inundating him with questions, he held up his hand and spoke, "Ladies and gentlemen, this is Mr. Sherlock Holmes, a specialist in this type of case. He has a few questions for you. As you can tell, we are underway again and you will all be delivered to Westminster. For now, your cooperation is appreciated."

"As I understand it," began Holmes, "only the men in this room and the crew have been asked to view the body in an attempt at identification. I, too, wish to spare the ladies that experience. For now, if I may speak to each of you gentlemen in private in the dining room, we should be quite finished before we reach Westminster."

The detective went into the adjoining room wherein the round tables were clear of tablecloths and bore a bright lustre to their mahogany surfaces. Inspector Carmichael invited each of the men in turn to sit with Holmes. The first to arrive was Dr. Samuel Yost, a renowned physician and newly elected Member of Parliament, having replaced his constituency's former Member of Parliament who had recently died.

Holmes looked the fellow over. His stout body showed signs of middle age, his cummerbund dipping with the excess weight accumulating around his waist. His hairline was receding, yet the hair itself was still of a deep brown that curled down his cheeks and into a thin moustache.

Holmes began. "I understand you do not know our victim, Doctor?"

The gentleman folded his hands upon the table and answered calmly, "I've never laid eyes on him before tonight, Mr. Holmes"

"Did all of you board the vessel together after the party, or did anyone arrive earlier than the others?"

"We left the party as a group. We passed through the palace doors, saying our farewells to the royal family as we exited. Each previous couple was perhaps fifty feet ahead, at most, before the next party finished their goodbyes and followed. I daresay no one was ever out of sight of at least one other couple at any time before we reached the boat."

Holmes nodded, "And after you boarded, did you all remain together?"

"Four of us stayed on deck until we were underway, enjoying the starlight. But the movement of the boat through the chill air soon drove us below to join the others."

"Who was below deck while you were stargazing?"

"Sir Carlton Lawson and his wife, Margaret, were there, along with Admiral and Mrs. Alston. He was the one who agreed with Captain Hunt and his decision to not tie up while the possibility of a murderer on board was evident."

Holmes checked the list Carmichael had provided, "That left Count Dressen and Lady Kirsten on deck with you, then?"

"Yes, though I don't know them well. We had only met tonight. He is a friend of Prince Arthur."

"Did you take a close look at the body, Doctor?"

"Just a cursory glance to verify he was dead. I would have done more, however, the Captain insisted on calling in the River Police."

"So, you formed no opinion as to the manner in which he died?"

"The stiffness of the body surprised me. That stage of *rigor mortis* would indicate the body had been there long before we boarded. That was my argument for moving on, since it obviously happened sometime earlier in the evening. Ha! Did you ever try arguing with an Admiral on board a ship, Mr. Holmes?"

"No one above the rank of captain," answered the detective, with a quick smirk. "I can only imagine the difficulty." He paused, checked his notes and declared, "Just one more thing, who requested the stewards to bring out more wine?"

Yost squinted at the question quizzically then replied, "I believe that was Lady Kirsten."

Holmes made a note and declared, "Very well, that's all I have for you for now, Doctor. I presume you will be returning home if the police need to reach you over the next few days?"

"Yes, Mr. Holmes. Though I can't think of anything else I could add."

"Thank you, sir." Holmes stood and shook the fellow's hand as he showed him to the door.

Before requesting the next witness, Holmes called Inspector Carmichael into a private conversation and made a request. The river policeman looked at him askance, but agreed to follow his instruction and left the room.

The next three interviews were much in the same vein. Count Dressen, a gentleman in his early thirties who walked with a slight limp due to a fall from a horse earlier in the year, was of even less help than Dr. Yost. He was polite, but rather the worse for drink. He kept insisting that a crewman must have done it while they were at the party.

Sir Carlton was a nervous sort of fellow. A small man of perhaps forty years. He kept glancing about at the slightest noise. When Holmes attempted to calm him, he sputtered, "Keep calm? How can I keep calm? How can any of us, knowing that there is a murderer on board? You must unmask the fellow, Mr. Holmes. None of us are safe until the Inspector makes an arrest!"

"I assure you, Sir Carlton, everyone is perfectly safe for the remainder of this trip. We are not dealing with a mass murderer. The victim was the only man targeted."

"How can you know that, Mr. Holmes?" he demanded.

"It is my business to know what other people do not," said the detective in his most reassuring tone. He dismissed the man and then spoke briefly with Admiral Alston.

"I appreciate your suggestion to bring this case to me, Admiral. May I ask what inspired you to do so? "

Alston, a large man in his fifties with grey mutton chop whiskers and moustache, standing tall in his naval dress uniform displaying a significant number of medals, merely replied, "A mutual acquaintance of ours at the Home Office has mentioned your talent for this sort of thing is nearly equal to his own. I knew he would not be amenable to being awoken so early, thus I felt you to be the next best option."

Holmes smiled briefly, "How kind of him. Have you yourself drawn any conclusions?"

"Only that I shall be speaking with the Captain of the Guard at Kew Palace. No one should have been able to board this vessel unnoticed."

Holmes thanked the Admiral and returned below to us. Drake and I had managed to move the body out of cold storage and into an anteroom where he was still out of sight of the passengers. Upon my friend's arrival, I spoke up, "See here, Holmes," I said, kneeling by the body. "Dr. Drake found this needle mark on the fellow's neck."

I pointed to a small mark on the left side of our victim's neck, behind the ear and about two inches below the temporal lobe. Holmes knelt, gave it a quick look, and noted, "A rather large bore needle, wouldn't you say, Dr. Drake?"

"Aye, Sherlock, t'was either a thick solution or the killer wanted to deliver a large dose as quickly as possible."

"A needle that large would certainly have been capped to prevent leakage," pondered the detective.

"Most certainly. It would have been capped in any case, but this one would have been larger than standard," replied the police surgeon. Drake's brow furrowed in thought as he stared at his former pupil. "What are you thinking, Sherlock?"

Holmes bowed his head, the front bill of his travelling cap nearly hiding his eyes from us. His right forefinger tapped his lips as his thumb tucked under his well-defined chin. He closed his eyes for roughly twenty seconds as we stood there, waiting for some pronouncement. At last, he opened his eyes, thrust his hands deep into his coat pockets and left us, calling back over his shoulder, "I must consult Inspector Carmichael and Captain Hunt. Excuse me gentlemen. I believe we shall soon run our prey to ground."

I looked at my medical colleague and he merely shrugged his shoulders and bowed to cover the body with a sheet from the boat's storage. I was dumbfounded, however. I had certainly seen Holmes make complex deductions and arrive at the truth over the short time we had lived together. Nonetheless, I could not see how the little bit of evidence this body yielded could lead to a specific conclusion. I could only assume some clue during his interviews had triggered that machine-like brain of his into forming a viable hypothesis. Dr. Drake apparently saw the consternation on my face and shook his head. "Don't bother to try and read Sherlock's mind, Doctor. His deductive reasoning power is far beyond anyone I've ever known. It will all seem quite logical when he explains it."

Chapter Four

Shortly before we were to arrive, Holmes, Carmichael, Drake and I met with the passengers who were still seated randomly around the lounge. Carmichael had surreptitiously stationed his officers just out of sight at each exit as a precautionary measure. Holmes stepped up and caught everyone's attention.

"Ladies and gentlemen, we will soon be at Westminster Pier and arranging transportation for each of you. In the meantime, I wished to inform you that we have identified our unfortunate victim."

I was determined to note the physical reactions of the passengers when Holmes made his announcement.

"The gentleman was a Frenchman named Henri Despereaux. He is not unknown to the Paris police and was wanted for questioning in several cases there regarding burglary and blackmail."

Try as they might, there was more than one strong reaction to this news. They ranged from indifference to raised eyebrows and sudden intakes of breath in anticipation. Dr. Yost seemed little perturbed by this revelation and remarked, "Congratulations, Mr. Holmes. I'm sure you will be able to work with the gendarmes to find your killer. Another Frenchman whom he was blackmailing? The French are so quick-tempered at that sort of thing."

Holmes looked at him and replied casually, "Yes, it is very likely that one of his blackmail victims killed him. Well then, we shall be tying up soon and be on our way to our appropriate destinations."

After a short while we finally came to Westminster Pier. The captain informed the passengers that transportation was being arranged for each couple and soon the Alstons and Lawsons were on their way. With just the Yosts and Dressens left behind, Holmes and Carmichael requested one final meeting with the gentlemen without their wives. I was allowed to attend while Dr. Drake arranged to move the body. When we were apart from the ladies, Holmes invited the Doctor and the Count to take a seat. Holmes remained standing as he leaned against a desk in the office we had appropriated. Carmichael and I stood by the door.

There was a long pause as Holmes contemplated his words. At last, he pulled an object from his pocket and held it up for all to see. Immediately, Dr. Yost's hand went to the pocket of his overcoat. Realizing what the detective had found and its implications, he leaned back in his chair and said, "Say what you have to say, Mr. Holmes."

My friend gazed at the object in his hand and replied, "Obviously, you recognize this as the cap for the syringe of poison which you used on Monsieur Despereaux. You absent-mindedly, no doubt, placed it in your pocket after you removed it to deliver the fatal dose to the man who was blackmailing your wife. I'm sure you tossed the syringe itself into the river, along with Despereaux's wallet, before you and the Count carried the body to the cold storage room below deck."

Count Dressen overcame his alcoholic haze and spoke, "How dare you, sir! That little cap is hardly proof of anything and certainly not of any involvement by me!"

Holmes replaced the cap into an envelope and handed it to Carmichael; as evidence. "Dr. Drake will be able to test this for traces of poison, Inspector. As to you, Count, your involvement is evident from two simple facts. After I determined that two men had moved the body into the storeroom, for such dead weight would be difficult for a single individual, I identified each of you by the marks left on your coats by the frosted surfaces you bumped against as you placed the body within. The very coats you are wearing now as you prepare to step out into the cold morning air. Second, your limp, sir, has caused you to drag your foot on occasion, especially when it is cold. Such drag marks were evident on the frosted floor in the storage compartment."

Reflexively, Dressen reached to the upper left sleeve of his coat and cursed his luck at what he found. Yost merely shook his head.

Holmes continued, "I was also able to observe which ladies had the strongest reaction when I announced the victim's identity. Both of your wives were quite remarkable, whereas the other women showed none or minimal interest only. Although I must congratulate you, Dr. Yost. You maintained a calm demeanour throughout. No doubt the years of practice at maintaining yourself under pressure through many difficult surgeries in your career."

Yost bowed his head in acknowledgment and replied, 'Not enough, I'm afraid. What happens now?"

Holmes folded his long arms across his chest, "There's been a murder, Doctor. Inspector Carmichael will have to detain you in that regard. You may have mitigating circumstances. That will be up to the magistrates to decide."

Carmichael spoke up, "I'm afraid you gentlemen and your wives will have to come with me and my men to Scotland Yard. There's a good many more questions to ask before we determine who and what to charge. I'm sure the Yard will wish to speak to you too, Mr. Holmes."

Holmes nodded and replied, "I shall come 'round this afternoon, Inspector and fill in any little gaps which I may for your report."

Carmichael and his men escorted the gentlemen and their wives off the boat to be taken to Scotland Yard. Holmes, Drake and I supervised the removal of the victim's body by the boat's crewmen to await a van for the mortuary. As we stood on the pier, the sun finally began to raise some heat as the breezes had subsided.

As we waited, Drake and I peppered Holmes with questions. "Tell me, Sherlock," asked the elderly physician, "Where did you come up with the victim's name?"

My friend craned his neck toward the sun, as he stretched his lean frame, then replied, "What you took to be a French tailor's label, I recognized as the name of the victim, himself, M. Despereaux a well-known French raconteur, who uses his infectious skills to worm his way into the hearts, and often the beds, of many a noblewoman. His reputation in Paris has soured of late, as he is rumoured to have added to his reputation a talent for blackmail. I was aware of his arrival in England some months ago, as Paris became too hot for him. I was expecting a client would eventually make their way to my door to put an end to his adventures this side of the Channel, but none had come forth as yet."

I asked a question of my own, attempting to make sense of my companion's reasoning. "What do you deduce as the sequence of events that brought our victim into the boat's cold storage? Why wouldn't they just throw him into the river?"

"My answer at this point, Watson, would be a conjecture of the most likely scenario. We shall have to extract the true course of events when we interview the prisoners later today. My current surmise is that Despereaux arranged meetings with both Yost and Dressen last evening. It is unlikely they were meant for the same time, but somehow they became aware that they were each in the same situation. Dr. Yost came prepared to put an end to the blackmailer with his syringe of poison. Delivering it was much easier with the Count's assistance. It probably happened on the deck, out of sight of any passing crewman or palace guard. I verified with Captain Hunt that all crew members were invited to the servants' party while the guests attended the main ball. Once the poison was delivered, the Doctor threw the syringe into the Thames as he went to assist Dressen with catching the body. Throwing the body overboard would create a splash that may have been heard. But, by using the paralytic agent to stiffen the muscles, they could slip the body into the cold storage area, where it would also conceal the true time of death. It is likely they thought that no one would be going in there until well after they tied up in Westminster. Perhaps they felt that it would be written off as an intruder who accidentally locked himself within and froze to death. Or, perhaps, Dr. Yost believed he would be called upon to determine the cause of death and that he could cover his tracks with a misleading diagnosis. Captain Hunt's attention to protocol foiled his plan."

I shook my head, "Dressen must have been beside himself when it was his own wife who requested more wine and caused the body to be discovered prematurely."

"Oh, I'm sure of it, Watson. Hence his over indulgence in alcohol this evening. He could not overrule Lady Kirsten, as she is not one to be dissuaded from her desires, a trait I'm sure Despereaux took full advantage of."

Drake commented, "I cannot believe an educated physician and gentleman like Dr. Yost could stoop so low as to commit murder."

Holmes stuffed his gloved hands deep into the pockets of his coat and replied, "In my study of past criminals and cases throughout history, I have found that doctors make the most fiendish killers. For all their education, they have the most formidable knowledge of how to deliver death in the most ingenious and inconspicuous ways, as well as the ego to believe themselves not only justified, but too clever to get caught."

In the pregnant pause which followed that statement, Holmes noted the looks which Dr. Drake and I were both giving him and added, "Present company excepted, of course."

EDITOR'S NOTE: This is where Watson's notes end. A newspaper clipping, dated several weeks after this adventure, indicated that Dr. Yost had resigned his Parliamentary position and was relocating to Australia.

A Sherlock Holmes Alphabet of Cases Volume Three (K to O)

5 Star Review by Deborah Lloyd for Readers' Favorite

Five intriguing cases solved by consulting detective Sherlock Holmes, and his roommate Dr. John Watson, comprise *A Sherlock Holmes Alphabet of Cases, Volume Three: K-O*, written by Roger Riccard. The stories take place during the early years of Holmes's career in the 1880s, through the first decades of the twentieth century. From the beginning, his keen observations and astute deductions captivate and challenge the reader. The plots vary greatly – these include an international plot; a leprechaun appearing on a college campus; missing Sousaphones; valuable origami creations. Dr. Watson brings his medical knowledge to cases and often becomes a partner in following a criminal, or engaging a person while Mr. Holmes searches a house.

The subtle clues embedded in descriptive texts and comments are simply delightful. The relationship between the two men is also fascinating to watch as they embark on being roommates at 221B Baker Street. The author has captured the time period well. There are many examples of this, but certainly the various attitudes towards women are portrayed accurately. The spoken language reflects the era, and yet it is easy to read, due to Roger Riccard's skillful writing. Each story is clear, with a smooth flow, even as Sherlock Holmes and Dr. Watson deal with different socio-economic classes, cultures and geographic locations. Roger Riccard has written a wonderful rendition of a classic hero in *A Sherlock Holmes Alphabet of Cases, Volume Three: K-O*. This book is highly recommended for anyone who loves a fun and interesting read and who is a Sherlock Holmes or historical detective story fan.

A Sherlock Holmes Alphabet of Cases Volume Four (P to T)

5 Star Review by Edith Wairimu for Readers' Favorite

In Roger Riccard's captivating *A Sherlock Holmes Alphabet of Cases Volume 4 (P-T)*, Holmes applies his ingenuity to solve some of the most puzzling cases. The collection comprises five cases. In the first, *The Piccadilly Poisoner*, one of Dr. Watson's patients shows signs of poisoning. Who could be behind the cruel crime? In the second, *The Dead Quiet Library*, two people are found dead in a quiet, eerie library that is said to be haunted by a ghost. In *The Raspberry Tart*, the third case, a banker is sceptical about his son's fiancée and wants an investigation that proves to his son he is about to make a dire mistake. In *The Student Olympian*, the fourth of Holmes's cases, a star rider suddenly withdraws from participating in the 1908 Olympics. While in the fifth, *Death on the Thames*, a body is found on the Royal Riverboat.

Creatively told, each case in *A Sherlock Holmes Alphabet of Cases Volume 4 (P-T)* by Roger Riccard combines humour and Sherlock Holmes's discernment to reach a surprising conclusion. Holmes's mannerisms are amusing and the friendship and resulting conversations he shares with Dr. Watson are also interesting. These Sherlock Holmes cases prove to be intricate and it is fascinating to read how the great detective examines the events surrounding each case and his discovery of the culprits. The characters are well-developed as each plays a significant role in the work. Innovative and entertaining, *A Sherlock Holmes Alphabet of Cases* is an amazing read for all fans of Sherlock Holmes detective stories.